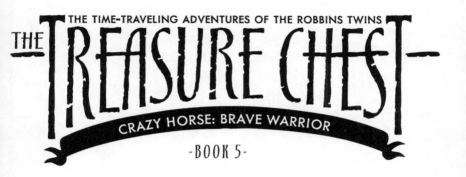

THE TIME-TRAVELING ADVENTURES OF THE ROBBINS TWINS

THE TREASURE CHEST

CRAZY HORSE: BRAVE WARRIOR

-BOOK 5-

BY *NEW YORK TIMES* BEST-SELLING AUTHOR
ANN HOOD

Grosset & Dunlap
An Imprint of Penguin Group (USA) Inc.

For Delila Dot

GROSSET & DUNLAP
Published by the Penguin Group
Penguin Group (USA) Inc., 375 Hudson Street, New York, New York 10014, USA
Penguin Group (Canada), 90 Eglinton Avenue East, Suite 700, Toronto, Ontario M4P 2Y3, Canada
(a division of Pearson Penguin Canada Inc.)
Penguin Books Ltd, 80 Strand, London WC2R 0RL, England
Penguin Ireland, 25 St Stephen's Green, Dublin 2, Ireland
(a division of Penguin Books Ltd)
Penguin Group (Australia), 707 Collins Street, Melbourne, Victoria 3008, Australia
(a division of Pearson Australia Group Pty Ltd)
Penguin Books India Pvt Ltd, 11 Community Centre, Panchsheel Park, New Delhi—110 017, India
Penguin Group (NZ), 67 Apollo Drive, Rosedale, Auckland 0632, New Zealand
(a division of Pearson New Zealand Ltd)
Penguin Books (South Africa), Rosebank Office Park, 181 Jan Smuts Avenue, Parktown North 2193, South Africa
Penguin China, B7 Jiaming Center, 27 East Third Ring Road North, Chaoyang District, Beijing 100020, China

Penguin Books Ltd, Registered Offices: 80 Strand, London WC2R 0RL, England

Text © 2013 by Ann Hood. Illustrations ©2013 by Penguin Group (USA) Inc. Published by Grosset & Dunlap, a division of Penguin Young Readers Group, 345 Hudson Street, New York, New York 10014. GROSSET & DUNLAP is a trademark of Penguin Group (USA) Inc. Printed in the U.S.A.

Library of Congress Cataloging-in-Publication Data is available.

Illustrations by Denis Zilbur. Map illustration by Giuseppe Castellano.
Design by Giuseppe Castellano.

ISBN 978-0-448-45728-4 (pbk)   10 9 8 7 6 5 4 3 2 1
ISBN 978-0-448-45738-3 (hc)   10 9 8 7 6 5 4 3 2 1

ALWAYS LEARNING   PEARSON

CHAPTER 1

Weeping Willows

If it can be said that a house mourns, then Elm Medona itself was as sad as Maisie and Felix. Without Great-Aunt Maisie, the rooms seemed darker and duller. The hallways yawned long and forlorn. Even the grounds, which should have been bursting with the first crocuses and daffodils of spring, refused to have the tight purple and yellow buds blossom. Ever since the funeral, it had rained. Hard.

"It's like the sky is crying," Felix had said, and even though Maisie had rolled her eyes and muttered, "Now he's a poet," she secretly agreed that everything around them was mourning.

Great-Uncle Thorne took to his room and refused

to come out. In the two weeks since Great-Aunt Maisie's funeral, he had taken all his meals in his room and kept his door firmly shut.

"I know what would make him feel better," Maisie said one night as she and Felix watched the maid carry a silver tray with his dinner out of the Kitchen. Three times a day the cook made Great-Uncle Thorne the exact same thing: *croque-monsieur*, which was really just a fancy ham-and-cheese sandwich; sliced cucumbers in sour cream; warm potato salad with bacon and mustard; and a single scoop of lemon sorbet with raspberry sauce.

Maisie and Felix were eating grilled cheese-and-tomato sandwiches at the big wooden table that was mostly used for preparing their meals. Since Great-Aunt Maisie died, it had felt too weird to resume eating in the Dining Room. Instead, they wandered in and out of the enormous basement kitchen, leaving half-eaten apples and toast crumbs on the counters.

Felix knew what Maisie meant: a visit to The Treasure Chest. When they went into The Treasure Chest and picked up an object, they traveled back in time. He and Maisie had met Clara Barton, Alexander Hamilton, and Pearl Buck—all of them children, too. But the last time they did it, Great-Uncle Thorne and Great-Aunt Maisie had gone with them. They'd landed in Coney Island at the turn of the twentieth century and met a young Harry Houdini. What Maisie and Felix didn't know was that their aunt had masterminded the trip, and that she intended to stay there. Staying back in time, they learned, meant dying in the present. And to Felix, that was enough time traveling for the rest of his life. He couldn't help but feel somewhat responsible for what had happened, and now there was no way to fix it. Great-Aunt Maisie was gone forever.

"You know," Maisie said, narrowing her eyes at him, "if we go to The Treasure Chest and go back in time, it makes Great-Uncle Thorne healthier. If we don't . . ."

She let her voice trail off so that Felix could fill in the blanks himself.

"He'll get older and frailer," Felix said. "Which is exactly what's supposed to happen."

"But it doesn't *have* to happen," Maisie said. She had a new, annoying habit of dipping her grilled cheese sandwich into mayonnaise, which she did before every bite.

"I don't think we should mess with the natural order of things," Felix said, averting his eyes. Mayonnaise made him queasy, and he couldn't watch his sister eating it on the outside of her sandwich like that.

Maisie dipped the final triangle of her sandwich into the crystal bowl of mayo, licking the drips from it before popping it into her mouth.

"Natural order of things?" she repeated with her mouth full. "Ever since you won class president you talk like a politician."

"Really? I thought I sounded like a poet," Felix said.

"Maybe you just sound like a dope," Maisie said, getting up from the tall stool with a loud scrape against the tiled floor.

Felix watched his sister stomp away. In the past, Maisie somehow had convinced him to do just about anything she wanted, including going into The Treasure Chest that very first time back in the summer. But he was not going to let her talk him into another trip there. He was, after all, president of the class, leading home-run hitter, and in general, a normal, ordinary person. That was good enough for him.

"Must you slam doors all the time?" her mother asked Maisie that night.

The answer was yes. Maisie wanted to stomp, slam, rattle, pound, clank, clump, jangle, crash, smash. Maisie wanted to be heard. But no one was listening.

Her mother stood in a black dress and high heels, wearing too much makeup and holding a shiny black clutch purse, ready to go out yet again with Bruce Fishbaum, the lawyer she worked for and the person whom she spent more and more time with.

"Really, Maisie," her mother said, "I don't know why you have to be so noisy."

"I don't know why you have to go out with Bruce Fishbaum practically every night," Maisie said, glaring.

But her mother had already walked to the window, and she peered out expectantly, as if at any minute Bruce Fishbaum would drive up and take her away.

"It's business," her mother said unconvincingly. "You know that. I'm lucky the Fishbaums like me enough to have me go to these client dinners."

Frustrated, Maisie stomped out of the room, across the foyer, and up the Grand Staircase. One good thing about living in a mansion was that when you made a lot of noise, it echoed.

Upstairs, she walked slowly past Felix's room, which was, of course, empty. Ever since he won the class-president election, he always had somewhere to be: after-school meetings, evening planning committees, socializing with his cabinet. And when he wasn't doing that, he had baseball practice or pizza parties or a million other dumb things. The phone seemed to always be ringing these days, and the person on the other end was always looking for Felix. *Got to run!* he'd say to Maisie, and indeed he would run—right past her, his backpack straps flying as he ran out the door into a waiting car filled with friends.

All while Maisie stood and watched.

Maisie could not remember a time when she had been so alone. When they lived in New York just last year (though sometimes it felt to her like that had been a million years ago) they did almost everything together. Their little group of friends had been just that: *their* friends. No one would have invited Felix over without Maisie; no one would have asked Maisie to do something without Felix. They were a team, a pair, inseparable. One name was never even uttered without the other. *MaisieandFelix*. As if they were one person.

But somehow, here in terrible Newport, Rhode Island, Maisie had turned invisible. To her classmates. To her mother. And worst of all, to Felix.

In the distance, Maisie heard Bruce Fishbaum's BMW pull up. She went into her room, the overly colorful Princess Room, which had been designed for Princess Annabelle of Nanuh, and threw herself onto the bed so hard that it groaned and creaked under her weight. Maisie stared up at the canopy that stretched from one ornately carved post to the other and longed for her twin bed back on Bethune Street with Felix in his matching one on the other side of the scrim.

Their father was an artist who had met their mother when he painted the sets one summer for a theater company in the Berkshires in Massachusetts where she performed. Maisie could list all of the plays: *The Sound of Music*, *The Music Man*, *My Fair Lady*, *Hello, Dolly!*, and *The Odd Couple*. She used to look at the programs, proud to see her mother's name on the cast lists. Her mother had played Marian the Librarian and Liesl and Cecily Pigeon. Starring roles. In her picture in those programs, she looks beautiful, all wide-eyed, her hair tumbling to her shoulders.

Now the sound of voices—Bruce Fishbaum's deep one and her mother's fake trill—floated up and Maisie grimaced. How had her mother gone from that fresh-faced, beautiful woman in love with a burly artist to this person? A lawyer in wrinkled suits and kitten heels? Dating someone who wore nautical ties and drove a fancy car?

"Maisie?" her mother called from downstairs.

In such an enormous mansion, even when a person shouted, her voice sounded thin and far away.

"We're off!"

We're off? Maisie thought. When had her mother and Bruce Fishbaum become a *we*?

She jumped off the bed and clomped down the long hallway to the top of the Grand Staircase, arriving just in time to see the giant front doors closing.

"Have a terrible time!" Maisie shouted.

But of course no one heard her.

Bitsy Beal, the queen bee of Felix's new group of friends, was having a party. A March Madness party. *Because*, Bitsy said, *doesn't everyone go a little mad in March?*

This was exactly the kind of thing Maisie and Felix would hate. Should hate. But in fact, it was all Felix could talk about. Bitsy Beal and her stupid March Madness party. As if Maisie couldn't be more miserable with her life, now there was this to contend with.

"It's a costume party!" Felix announced over breakfast, as if this was the most brilliant idea ever.

Their mother was moping over her third cup of coffee, looking as miserable as Maisie felt.

"How fun," she said, trying to sound enthusiastic but missing by a lot.

"What's wrong with you?" Maisie asked her.

But her mother just shook her head and gave a small sigh.

"I think I'm going to go as the Mad Hatter," Felix said, not noticing that everyone around him couldn't care less.

"What a great idea," their mother said. She had

mascara smudges under her eyes and looked vaguely raccoonish.

"How was your date last night?" Maisie asked.

"We're just friends, Maisie," her mother said, staring into her coffee.

"Wait," Maisie said. "Did Bruce Fishbaum break up with you?"

"You can't break up with someone who's just your friend, can you?" she said angrily. With that, she practically ran out of the room.

Felix was writing a list. "I'll need a top hat," he said. "Green, I think. And a yellow tuxedo jacket."

"Seriously?" Maisie said, grabbing the pen out of his hand.

"Hey!"

"All you can think about is your stupid costume for Bitsy Beal's stupid party? Didn't you notice that Bruce Fishbaum dumped Mom last night?"

Felix looked around the kitchen as if he had just realized their mother was gone.

"He did?"

"Yeah," Maisie said. "Apparently."

"But that's a good thing, right?" Felix said. "We don't like Bruce Fishbaum."

Maisie blinked at her brother. "What did you say?"

"We don't like Bruce Fishbaum, do we?" Felix said.

Maisie grinned at Felix.

"Right," she said.

"All right then. May I have my pen back?"

Maisie handed Felix his pen, still grinning.

"You're being weird," Felix said, frowning at his list.

But Maisie didn't care. He had said it himself. Despite Bitsy Beal and her dumb party and baseball and everything, Maisie and Felix were still a *we*.

Everyone was surprised that night when, as they sat in the Library eating pizza their mother brought home from That's Amore, Great-Uncle Thorne appeared in the doorway. With his mane of white hair uncut these past few weeks, and his voluminous white eyebrows pointing in every direction, and his great, drooping white mustache and goatee, and his flowing silk smoking jacket, he took up the entire doorway. In one hand he gripped a walking stick with a shiny silver carved top, and the other hand flailed about like a conductor conducting an orchestra.

"What are you doing?" Great-Uncle Thorne bellowed.

Before any of them could answer, he bellowed some more.

"Eating? Pizza? In the LIBRARY?"

Their mother jumped to her feet, grabbing their plates and unceremoniously dumping their half-eaten pizza slices back into the box, which gaped open on one of the specially carved brass tables Phinneas Pickworth had brought back from India. Or Egypt. Somewhere special and far away.

"We do NOT eat in the LIBRARY!" Great-Uncle Thorne boomed.

"I am so sorry," their mother was saying as she scurried around, scraping crumbs and wiping at the table.

"That table was made by nomads!" Great-Uncle Thorne continued. "Berbers! Carved in the heat of the Sahara!"

Maisie and Felix stared down at the table, which they had never paid much attention to before. But now Felix saw that there was a story carved there. Intricate camels and men in turbans walking across a desert. Dunes rose behind them. Around the table, where Maisie sat, there were tents and food, a fire with a pot on it, and thin lines of steam etched into the brass.

"Sorry," Felix said. "It's beautiful," he added.

"Of course it's beautiful, you dolt. Phinneas Pickworth would not carry something that wasn't beautiful over three thousand miles," Great-Uncle Thorne said, striding into the room. He looked around, his eyes wild, as if searching for more infractions.

"The Dining Room just seems so empty," their mother said.

Great-Uncle Thorne frowned down at her.

"I have been waiting for the willow trees to weep for my sister," he said, his voice finally gentler. "And I have come down to announce that they have."

"The willow trees are—" their mother began.

"Weeping! That's what they do. Weeping willows, you ninny." He shook his head in disgust. "Maisie was right," he muttered. "She said you were a bunch of nincompoops."

"But trees don't feel anything," their mother insisted.

"Ha!" Great-Uncle Thorne said. "Come with me."

He began to walk out of the room, but turned around when he realized they weren't following him.

"Hup to now," he said.

Maisie, Felix, and their mother all quickly joined him.

"Willows don't weep," Great-Uncle Thorne said incredulously under his breath as he led them out the front doors, across the wide circular driveway, over the damp lawn, to the eastern side of Elm Medona.

There, a line of a dozen willow trees stood. And every one of them seemed bent in grief. Their branches, covered in pale green newly blossomed leaves, brushed the ground beneath them. A slight breeze blew, making the branches sway. The sight of twelve majestic trees mourning stopped all of them in their tracks.

"Listen," Great-Uncle Thorne ordered.

They listened.

Indeed, the sound of faint weeping filled the air.

"When our mother died, Phinneas said the willows wept for the entire month," Great-Uncle Thorne said.

Maisie thought it was surely just the wind rustling through the branches that made that sound.

But Felix stared up at the giant trees and believed in that moment that they were actually weeping for Great-Aunt Maisie.

Above the line of willows, a full moon rose. The night was so clear that soon stars littered the sky, twinkling brightly. Eventually, one by one, Maisie and Felix and their mother went back inside, shivering in the March chill. But Great-Uncle Thorne stayed outside, weeping beside the willow trees, long into the night.

CHAPTER 2

Lemonade M

One week before Bitsy Beal's March Madness party, the weather suddenly turned warm and balmy. Everyone started showing up at school in shorts and polo shirts the color of Easter eggs. That Tuesday morning, Felix appeared in the Kitchen in his old madras shorts and a lavender polo shirt, his backpack slung over one shoulder. On his feet were a pair of Top-Siders, those ugly boat shoes just about everybody in Newport wore, that Maisie had never seen before. He shoved a piece of toast into his mouth and gulped down a glass of orange juice, ignoring Maisie, who watched him the whole time.

"Why are you staring at me?" Felix finally said.

He didn't look at her when he spoke. Instead, he

worked on choosing a banana without any brown spots or any hints of green. Felix only liked perfect bananas, which were very hard to come by.

"I am staring at you because you look weird," Maisie said.

At this, Felix paused, a banana in each hand, and stared back at his sister.

His eyes began at the top of Maisie, which was her unruly, tangly, not-quite-blond hair, and slowly moved downward: a faded black T-shirt from the play *A Chorus Line* with cracked gold foil letters and silhouettes of dancers holding top hats; jeans, also faded; lime-green Jack Purcells with yellow shoelaces on one sneaker and white shoelaces with tiny rainbows on the other.

"*I* look weird?" he said.

Maisie followed his gaze down to her shoes.

"The rainbows," she said, "are meant to be ironic."

Felix shrugged and went back to inspecting the bananas.

Just yesterday during lunch, Avery Mason, who was famous for her hair, had leaned over and whispered, "Felix, how could you be twins with someone so strange?"

And Felix's heart had done a strange, confused tumble. He knew he should stick up for his sister. He should tell Avery Mason that Maisie wasn't strange, just eccentric. He should defend her unique character, explain that once you got to know her, you would be impressed by how smart she was and excited by her adventurous spirit.

But instead, he had said, "Maybe they mixed up the babies at the hospital." After he said it, his mouth tasted like chalk.

Now Felix sighed and rejected both bananas.

"I mean," Maisie was saying, "you have a shirt with a pony on it."

Felix chose to ignore her. He began to examine the oranges in the bowl on the counter. A perfect orange was more soft than hard, but not too soft.

"And it's purple," she said.

"Uh-huh," Felix said, because why argue about clothes of all things? Especially when he understood that Maisie wasn't really mad about his shirt. She was jealous that he had friends. Lots of them. And that he won the student council election. And that he liked living in Newport. A lot. Maisie had chosen to keep one foot in the past, but Felix had decided to live very much in the present.

"You look," she said slowly, "ridiculous."

"Duly noted," Felix said. He squeezed an orange. This might be the right one.

Their mother appeared in one of her rumpled business suits. She looked, Maisie thought, determined.

"Good morning," she said brightly. "How about a ride to school?"

"What are you up to?" Maisie said.

"Can't I give you a ride to school without being up to something?" she said, rolling her eyes. "So cynical, my daughter is."

"As usual, everyone is picking on me," Maisie said loudly. "Relentlessly."

In language arts yesterday, Mrs. Witherspoon had told them that adverbs were a sign of weak writing, so Maisie had decided to use as many adverbs as possible.

Her mother narrowed her eyes. "Where in the world did you dig out that old thing?" she said, pointing to the T-shirt Maisie wore.

"In the giveaway box," Maisie said. "I can't believe all the great stuff you were thoughtlessly planning on sending off to Goodwill."

Her mother waved her hand as if she were sweeping things away. "Be my guest," she said.

She glanced at her watch and announced if they wanted a ride, they had to leave.

"I accept," Maisie said. "Gratefully."

Felix groaned. Why couldn't Maisie be even a little bit normal?

"So," their mother said as she drove down Bellevue Avenue, "I'm having dinner with Bruce Fishbaum tonight. And I will be very late."

Her eyes darted nervously to the rearview mirror, then back to the road.

She cleared her throat.

"This dinner," she said, then she cleared her throat again.

Maisie elbowed Felix hard in the ribs. He was looking over his math homework and hardly paying attention.

"Ow!" he said, and elbowed her back.

"Can you two please pay attention to what I'm about to say?" their mother said.

"Oh, I'm paying attention," Maisie said. She

searched for the perfect adverb. "Attentively," she said finally.

"Paying attention attentively?" Felix repeated. "That's redundant. And besides, Miss Landers says that adverbs are the weakest part of speech. You don't whisper softly. Whispers are soft."

"I love adverbs," Maisie said. "I adore them."

"You don't yell loudly," Felix continued. "Yelling is loud."

The brick front of Anne Hutchinson Elementary School appeared down the block.

"I'm trying to tell you that Bruce Fishbaum is officially not my friend anymore," their mother practically shouted.

With that, she pulled over to the side of the road, slammed on the brakes, and brought the Mustang to a screeching halt.

Maisie and Felix were stunned into silence.

"Mom," Felix said finally, "isn't it going to be kind of awkward working with someone who's not your friend?"

Their mother turned around in her seat so that she was facing them full-on.

"Well," she said, and then she got a funny look

on her face. She half smiled, and her eyes got dreamy and moist. "He's not my friend, because he's now my boyfriend."

Maisie and Felix stared back at their mother, who looked suddenly young and girlish, in a way that made them both feel uncomfortable.

"What about Dad?" Felix asked.

"Although he's your father, he's my ex-husband," their mother said evenly. "I am allowed, even entitled, to have a boyfriend."

That weird half smile came back and she said, "And I do. Have one. A boyfriend, I mean."

Her cheeks grew pink, and her eyes grew dreamier.

"Bruce," she said as if the name itself was magical. "Bruce is my boyfriend."

Felix could only stare at this person who was acting and sounding and looking nothing like his mother.

But Maisie moved into action. She unbuckled her seat belt and snapped the door open. She grabbed her backpack and, her eyes blazing, she announced, "I will never speak to you again, you . . . you . . . traitor!"

Then she got out of the car and stomped down the street toward school.

"Felix?" their mother said. "You understand, don't you?"

Felix wanted to say yes. But his mind was full of all the things it meant to have a boyfriend. It meant his mother spending time with that boyfriend and holding his hand and kissing him. Those were the things his mother did with his father. And now she was doing them with Bruce Fishbaum.

"I'm sorry," he said finally. "I don't."

The school bell rang, and Felix slowly gathered his things.

"He's wonderful," his mother said. "Just wait until you get to know him."

Felix just shook his head and got out of the car. Up ahead, Maisie had already disappeared into the crowd of kids going into school. Felix hurried to catch up.

Ever since Great-Aunt Maisie died, Felix found himself liking the escape of school and all its activities more than being in Elm Medona. For a brief time, after Great-Uncle Thorne had moved them out of the servants' quarters and into the mansion itself, being at home had seemed like a mysterious adventure. Even though Felix felt weird having maids and cooks and a butler, he still liked eating at the enormous Dining Room table on the Pickworth china and doing homework in the Library, with its burgundy leather walls and bookshelves lined with first editions of books by writers like Mark Twain and Nathaniel Hawthorne and Emily Dickinson.

But now it seemed to Felix that everywhere he looked in Elm Medona reminded him of Great-Aunt Maisie. At school, the smells of chalk dust and floor wax and sweat comforted him. He liked sitting around the table with the other class officers—Lily and Bitsy and Avery and Jim—discussing replacing the snacks in the vending machines with healthier choices and when to hold a car wash to raise money for the class trip to Washington, DC, and what the theme of the sixth-grade dance should be. Sometimes, Lily Goldberg caught him staring at her and smiled. That was always a good thing. He liked baseball practice, changing into his red-and-white uniform and running out to the field behind the school. And he liked walking home in the late afternoon with Jim Duncan, who would tell Felix the elaborate plots of the most recent postapocalyptic novel he'd read, or describe the physics of how a sailboat sailed.

This afternoon, with the knowledge of his mother going out with her *boyfriend*, Felix wished he didn't have to go home at all. The class officers were having a planning session for the dance. Avery and Bitsy wanted the theme to be "All You Need Is Love." Jim and Felix wanted it to be *Starlight Express* (Felix's idea—his mother had been in the road show of it a long time ago and played the sound track a lot). And Lily was arguing for "Up, Up and Away."

"We can have balloons everywhere and stars on the ceiling—" she was saying, when from the doorway, Maisie hissed, "Felix!"

Everyone turned to face her.

"This is the executive committee meeting," Bitsy said.

Maisie glared at her.

"Which means it's private," Avery added.

Felix saw the look that swept over Maisie's face, the one that she got when she was trying not to cry.

"I'll see you at home in a while," he said.

"I thought we could walk home together," Maisie said.

"We're not done here," Avery said, tossing her beautiful hair.

"Felix?" Maisie said, her voice sounding small.

Felix hesitated. Part of him wanted to adjourn the meeting and leave with his sister. He knew she was as upset as he was about what their mother had told them. They could maybe even stop for pizza at That's Amore and delay going home until their mother and Bruce Fishbaum were long gone. But part of him knew that if he left now, his friends would think he was a wimp. They already thought Maisie was weird, and that Felix gave in to her unreasonable demands too often. He was enjoying his status as a popular kid. Why did Maisie have to ruin everything?

"I'll see you at home later," he said softly.

Maisie's eyes widened. "But—"

Felix looked away from her because he knew if he looked at her he wouldn't have the strength to stay. "I think you were explaining your idea, Lily?"

"Uh, right," Lily said. "So balloons and stars and—"

"That's a stupid, boring idea," Maisie said. "It's . . . it's . . . a cliché!"

Everyone stared down at their hands, uncomfortable. Slowly, Felix raised his eyes to his sister. Weren't eyes supposed to be the windows to the soul? Hadn't Shakespeare or someone said that? Felix willed all of his feelings into his eyes, begging Maisie to understand why he couldn't leave with her.

Instead, Maisie's eyes seemed to be trying to tell him something, too. He saw the hurt in them, and the embarrassment, but still he didn't get up to leave. Instead, he just shook his head. Everyone thought twins understood absolutely everything about each other, but in this case, neither of them seemed to understand the other. In that endless moment, a terrible thought struck Felix: He didn't want to be a twin anymore. He wanted to be just him, Felix Robbins.

He watched Maisie as she slowly turned away and walked off down the hall. Even though Lily was talking about glow-in-the-dark stars, Felix didn't turn back to her until his sister disappeared.

When Felix finally did get home, Maisie was in

her room with the door shut.

"Hey," he said through the closed door, "want to make some popcorn?"

She didn't answer.

"Look, we had to vote on a theme," he said.

Nothing.

"You're going to like it," he told her. "It's *Starlight Express.*"

Felix waited, but Maisie didn't open the door or answer him. With a sigh, he went into his own room, Samuel Dormitorio, flopped onto the bed, and stared at the bull's head that hung on the wall opposite him. The room, with its abundance of weapons and dead animals, used to give him the creeps. But all of his friends thought it was the coolest room they'd ever seen, and that having a room named for a Spanish duke was even cooler. Somehow, that made Samuel Dormitorio slightly less creepy.

But this afternoon, the bull seemed to be looking at Felix accusingly.

"I have a life, you know," he said to the bull's head. "We're not conjoined twins. We're not even identical twins."

His door flew open, startling Felix enough for him to let out a yelp.

"Felix," Maisie said, ignoring the fact that he had not only yelped but also jumped off the bed, "you have got to come in my room."

"Oh," Felix said, "*now* you want me to come in your room. Never mind that I stood out there forever and you wouldn't even answer me."

Maisie was already on her way back out, though. Felix sighed and started to follow her. But then he stopped. Was he going to spend his entire life following his sister whenever she said to? His friends were right: Maisie was always bossing him around. And he always let her. If he was going to stand on his own and be just Felix Robbins, an un-twin, didn't he have to stop doing everything just because Maisie told him to?

"Hurry up!" Maisie called to him.

Well, he decided, he owed it to her, at least this once.

The hallway was empty when he stepped into it. Felix walked extra slowly, just to make a point. Inside the Princess Room, there was no sign of Maisie. Felix stood in the middle of the room and called her name.

"In here," she answered from the closet.

Felix walked across the room to the big walk-in closet where Maisie waited. She had pushed her few dresses over to one side, and stood with her arms folded in the middle of the closet.

"So I came in here to see if I had anything for my costume," Maisie began.

"Costume?" Felix asked.

"For Bitsy's stupid party," Maisie said. "March Madness."

Felix's stomach dropped, like he was on a roller coaster heading down.

"I was thinking March Madness, March Madness," Maisie continued. "And then it came to me. I could dress like Jo March."

"Uh-huh," Felix said.

"You know, from *Little Women*. All I would need is an old-fashioned dress and stuff, and I remembered that there was a trunk of dresses in here just like that, so I came in here and . . ."

Maisie paused. Her brother's face was white, and he didn't seem to be listening to her at all.

"What?" she said. "I think it's clever."

Felix nodded. "It is clever," he said.

They looked at each other. The air in the closet was stale and smelled vaguely of lavender.

"Anyway," Maisie said carefully, "I opened the trunk."

She demonstrated, lifting the heavy lid.

"And look what I found."

Felix tried to be interested. But all he could think about was the fact that Maisie was not invited to Bitsy Beal's party. How could she even think she was, when she hadn't received one of the fancy invitations Bitsy had mailed? They came in large pale-green envelopes—when you opened them, cherry blossoms fell out. Her father had paid a nursery a fortune to force cherry trees to bloom just so Bitsy could put the blossoms in the invitations.

"Well?" Maisie said. "What do you think it means?"

She stood in front of the open trunk, pointing to the lavender silk that lined it.

Felix went to stand beside her. He tried to focus on the squiggles in front of him, but his mind raced with ways to finagle an invitation for Maisie.

"Why would someone write all that?" Maisie demanded.

Felix adjusted his glasses and looked more closely, forcing himself to pay attention.

There, in beautiful penmanship and with black ink, someone had written:

Elm Medona   Lemonade m

Madelon me   Almond mee

Omland eem   Mamelon dee

"Well," Felix said, "it's gibberish."

"No, it's not," Maisie said, pointing to the top line. "Elm Medona? That's not gibberish."

"Okay," Felix admitted. "But *Mamelon dee* is. And *Omland eem*."

"I think it means something," Maisie insisted.

"Lemonade m?" Felix said.

Maisie lifted the folded dresses that filled the trunk to reveal the lavender silk lining beneath them.

"How about all of this then?" she asked him.

Felix peered inside.

Hundreds of similar phrases were written there, filling the entire inside of the trunk.

"Whose trunk was this?" Felix wondered.

Maisie shrugged.

"I think it's a code or something," she said.

Felix tried to make sense of any of it. After every few dozen, the person had written Elm Medona again, then more of the nonsensical phrases.

"I don't know," he said. "Why did they keep writing Elm Medona?"

"It reminds me of that day Great-Aunt Maisie made us try to crack the code for the Fabergé egg, remember?"

"Of course I remember. *Metaphoric kiwis* was an anagram for Maisie Pickworth," Felix said.

They both looked up from the words they'd been staring at.

"Anagrams!" Maisie said, excited. Just as she had suspected all along! "These are anagrams for Elm Medona!"

CHAPTER 3

Penelope Merriweather

"Maybe we could ask Great-Uncle Thorne?" Felix said.

This was much later, after Maisie had dutifully read aloud each entry and they'd both decided that whoever had tried to crack the anagram had not succeeded. None of them made any sense or led to anything even remotely interesting or revelatory. They'd puzzled over the anagram themselves, each of them writing the words Elm Medona on a piece of paper and then rearranging the letters the entire time they ate dinner. The cook had left roasted chicken and French fries—Cook insisted they call them *frites*, which they both found ridiculous—for them, and they'd sat together in that enormous

Kitchen, nibbling and writing and thinking.

Maisie did not want to ask Great-Uncle Thorne. In fact, she didn't want to involve him at all. Finding the writing in that trunk had been just the thing to bring Felix back into her orbit. He was finally paying attention to her again. Once they told someone else, she would become the third wheel again. And Maisie was sick of being the third wheel.

"I don't know," she said, dipping a fry into mayonnaise, which Cook approved of; apparently everyone in France dipped their *frites* in mayo. "I think we can solve this if we just stick to it."

Felix looked doubtful.

"Maybe we're missing something," Maisie said.

"Obviously," Felix said with a sigh.

He chewed the eraser of his pencil, an old habit that he'd mostly lost. It made Maisie feel nostalgic watching him. She remembered when all the pencils in his pencil box had gnawed bottoms. Their second-grade teacher, Miss Lupa, had put Tabasco on his pencils, and when their father found out, he'd gone to the school and demanded she be fired. Of course she wasn't. But Maisie and Felix had enjoyed the drama of their burly father in his paint-splattered clothes defending Felix's right to chew his pencils.

"What are you smiling about?" Felix asked.

"Miss Lupa," Maisie said.

"The pencils," Felix said, nodding.

"Remember when Dad said, 'Who's named Lupa anyway? It means *wolf*!'"

Felix walked over to the giant stainless-steel refrigerator and peered inside.

"There's chocolate pudding," he reported.

"Yum," Maisie said happily.

"Except, of course, Cook calls it *pot au chocolat*," Felix said as he brought two ramekins of pudding and two spoons to the table.

"She has a French name for everything," Maisie said.

"Great-Uncle Thorne does it, too," she added. She took a taste of the thick chocolate pudding. "Mmmm," she said. "Heavenly."

"And Great-Aunt Maisie. The whole lot of them throw French words into everything they say."

"*Bon appétit!*" Maisie said, imitating the way Great-Aunt Maisie used to speak.

"*À demain!*" Felix said with a giggle.

"*Pourquoi!*" Maisie said.

"*Mon dieu!*" Felix said.

Maisie looked at her brother.

"Elm Medona," she said.

"That's not French," Felix said.

"Maybe," Maisie said, studying the anagrams she'd written.

"What are you thinking?" Felix asked.

He looked down at his own anagrams. None of them made any sense.

"Wait a minute. Do you think Elm Medona is an anagram for a French word?" he asked suddenly.

"Well," Maisie said, "it sure isn't an anagram for an English one."

Felix seemed to be concentrating really hard on something.

"What?" Maisie asked impatiently.

"I know you won't want to do it," he said.

"Spit it out already," Maisie said.

"Avery Mason speaks fluent French," Felix said. "She went to a French American school until last year."

"No," Maisie said.

"I told you that you wouldn't want to do it. Even though she might be able to help us."

"Well," Maisie said, considering.

"All we have to do is have her look at the trunk."

"Well," Maisie said again.

"Or our lists," Felix offered. "We could go to her house right now. It'll take an hour, tops."

When Maisie didn't say anything, Felix said, "Or I could go by myself."

"No!" Maisie said quickly.

She was not about to lose Felix again so soon after she'd gotten him back.

"I'll go with you," she said reluctantly, because what else could she say?

Despite their mother's insistence that they never ask Charles the chauffeur to drive them anywhere, they had both readily decided that since their mother was out on a *date* with her *boyfriend*, they could do whatever they wanted. Maisie enjoyed pushing the button that beckoned Charles to the mansion. And she liked how quickly he responded, walking into the foyer already dressed in his black chauffeur uniform with his cap pulled low on his forehead.

"Miss Robbins?" he said, as cool and calm as if she beckoned him every day.

"We need to go somewhere," Maisie said.

"Yes, Miss," Charles answered.

Felix gave him the address, and in no time they were sitting in the backseat of the black limousine, cruising down Bellevue Avenue, grinning at each other.

Avery Mason lived in a big, sprawling house that sat on a long spit of land that stretched out into the ocean.

"Creepy," Maisie pronounced when they arrived.

"Wait here for us, please," Felix said as he got out of the limo.

"Yes, Master Robbins," Charles said.

"He's like a robot," Felix whispered to Maisie on their way to the front door.

"He's just a professional, that's all," Maisie said, as if she knew all there was to know about chauffeurs.

Avery opened the door before they even rang the bell.

"What's this French emergency?" she asked, letting them inside.

Her house was the complete opposite of Elm Medona—modern, all glass and sharp angles, open spaces, and cathedral ceilings.

"We're playing this . . . um . . . game," Felix said. "And we need to find anagrams."

"That's when you reorder letters to make a new word or phrase," Maisie explained.

Avery looked at her like she was a total moron. "I know what an anagram is," Avery said, tossing her beautiful hair.

"But we think this one is in French," Felix said. "And you are fluent in French."

"Mais oui," Avery said perfectly.

She led them into a large room with one entire wall made of glass that overlooked the water. Waves crashed onto the rocks below and an almost full moon hung above them. All the furniture was white, which made Maisie uncomfortable, like she was going to get it dirty somehow.

Once they'd settled onto separate white chairs, Felix handed Avery their lists.

"The anagram is for Elm Medona?" Avery said.

Felix nodded.

"What kind of game is this?" Avery asked.

But she went to work right away, moving her lips as she read to herself.

"I can't really find one," she said after a long time.

Maisie sighed with disappointment.

"That's okay," Felix said. "Thanks for trying."

"Anything for you, F," Avery said.

F? Maisie thought grumpily.

Felix grinned. "I appreciate it, A."

"Oh, please," Maisie muttered as the two of them giggled together.

Avery led them back to the front door, where she handed Felix the papers.

"You know what's funny?" she said when they stepped outside. "One of the anagrams is *lame demon.*"

"I found that one," Maisie said.

"Le diable boiteux," Avery said in perfectly accented French.

"What's funny about a lame demon?" Felix asked.

"Well, not funny really, but curious. You know, it's from that French book," Avery said.

"We don't know," Maisie said. Here was Avery, bragging as usual. Standing there in her glass house with her beautiful hair and some kind of classical music playing in another room and the waves crashing dramatically like she lived on a movie set.

"Paris Before Man? By Pierre Boitard?" Avery was saying.

Felix shook his head and shrugged helplessly.

"It's about time travel," Avery said.

Felix and Maisie looked at each other.

In the background, like they really were in a movie, the music hit a crescendo.

"*Lame demon*," Felix said softly.

"An anagram for Elm Medona," Maisie said just as softly.

Just then, the lights in Avery's house blinked once. Twice. Then they went out, leaving the three of them standing in total darkness. Avery gasped. But Maisie reached out into the black, found her brother's hand, and squeezed it. To her great relief and delight, Felix squeezed back.

"Isn't it weird that the lights went out *before* the storm arrived?" Maisie said as Charles drove them through the dark streets back to Elm Medona.

Felix squinted out at the blackness. He could not find a single light anywhere. It looked as if all of Newport had lost electricity. Rain pelted the windshield, and the wind blew so hard that he could actually feel it tugging on the limousine. Already branches had been ripped from trees and were being tossed around in the streets.

"Lame demon," Maisie said, and rested her head back against the long seat.

Slowly they drove along Bellevue Avenue, each mansion as dark as the next. They looked like museums, Felix thought as he stared out the window. He supposed in a way they were museums of the Gilded Age. Of a long-ago time. A shiver ran through him as he thought of all the people who had built them and held parties and danced in the fancy ballrooms. Not many of them were still lived in.

The car turned up the long driveway to Elm Medona, which loomed ahead of them.

Felix blinked.

"Look," he said, pointing out the window.

Maisie leaned over to see what he was pointing at.

Somewhere upstairs, one light shone. All around them, Newport was in darkness. In fact, Elm Medona was dark, too. Except one small light.

"Is that in Samuel Dormitorio?" Maisie asked.

In his mind's eye, Felix pictured the layout of the second floor, imagining each room.

"No," he said.

The limo was in the circular driveway now, its

tires splashing through puddles as it moved toward the entrance.

"Ariane's Bedroom?" Maisie asked, craning her neck to better see.

"No, that's on the other side," Felix said.

They had stopped. Charles stepped out into the rain and opened the door for them to exit. He held an enormous black umbrella for them to step under, and Maisie and Felix huddled beneath it, running inside.

The staff had lit giant pillar candles everywhere. They flickered and sent long shadows across the floors and walls.

Slowly, Maisie and Felix made their way upstairs. The air smelled of wax and some spicy scent.

"This must be what it was like here before they got electricity," Maisie said, her voice hushed.

Felix could only nod. He didn't like this storm, and he didn't like the way the shadows moved.

And he didn't like that now that they were upstairs, he couldn't see a single light on.

The door to the Aviatrix Room flew open and in the doorway stood their mother, her hair loose, her nightgown glowing eerily in the candlelight.

"Were you two out in this?" she said, her eyes blazing.

"When did you get home?" Felix asked.

"It's a genuine nor'easter out there," their mother said. "Came out of nowhere and it's wreaking havoc all over. Bruce and I were having a lovely dinner on Thames Street, and they made us evacuate."

At the sound of the name *Bruce*, Maisie decided to stomp off to her own room.

"Be careful of the candles," her mother called after her.

Felix looked at his mother. She was pretty in the candlelight, which made her face glow and soften.

"Were you two out somewhere?" she asked him.

"No," he said.

She narrowed her eyes.

"You're wet," she said.

Felix looked down at his wet clothes.

"We stepped outside to see if anybody else had electricity," he lied.

His mother kept staring at him for a long minute. Then she shook her head and turned to go back in her room.

"Mom?" Felix asked.

She paused.

"Is Bruce Fishbaum still your boyfriend?"

"Yes," she said gently.

Felix sighed, a long, sad one. Then he followed the path the candles lit for him back to his room.

Even though the next morning arrived sunny and bright, school was cancelled. Debris littered the streets of Newport, and two-thirds of the city still didn't have electricity. Felix and Maisie sat in the Dining Room eating croissants and trying to figure out what to do with their freedom.

"Maybe we could take a little trip," Maisie said, her eyes sparkling. She spread some strawberry jam on her croissant and took a big, sweet bite.

At first Felix didn't know what she meant. He was too busy separating the flaky layers of the pastry and eating each thin one before moving on to the next.

"*Lame demon,*" Maisie said.

"No," Felix said when he realized his sister wanted to go into The Treasure Chest.

"Wasn't Phinneas Pickworth clever?" Maisie said as if Felix hadn't spoken. "Not just an anagram but an anagram from a French book about time travel. Anyone could figure it out, really."

"We didn't," Felix grumbled. "Avery Mason did."

Maisie spread extra jam on her next piece of croissant, as if that could take away the bad taste in her mouth for all things Avery Mason. "She's a snob."

"She helped us," Felix reminded his sister.

"Inadvertently," Maisie said, happy to use both an adverb and a vocabulary word from last week's list.

"Don't those look good?" their mother purred as she came into the Dining Room.

Great-Uncle Thorne had decided that they absolutely had to stop eating in the Kitchen. "Pickworths don't dine in the basement!" he'd roared earlier that morning. Cook had scurried to move breakfast upstairs, setting up everything on the sideboard, which was really just a long table against the far wall.

"And isn't it nice to have everything laid out like this?" she added as she floated over to the sideboard and poured a cup of coffee from a silver pot with two interlocking *P*s etched into it.

"Oh, cubes of sugar!" she said, as if cubes of sugar were a marvel.

When she took a seat across from Maisie, Maisie saw that her mother was dressed for work. She had on a khaki-colored suit with a faint stain on the jacket lapel.

"Mom," Felix said, "Newport is basically closed."

"Not Fishbaum and Fishbaum," she said in her new, happy voice. She picked at some fresh fruit, all of it cut into exactly equal-size pieces. "Mmmm. How did Cook find such delicious strawberries in March?"

"I had them flown in from Guatemala," Great-Uncle Thorne roared. "Pickworths do not eat flaccid fruit."

"They are delicious," their mother said dreamily. Then, "Well, I've got to get to the office."

She had on lipstick and some kind of blush that made it look like she had a slight tan. Maisie studied her more closely. Her mother actually kind of sparkled.

The three of them watched her drift out of the room.

"What's wrong with her?" Great-Uncle Thorne asked Felix and Maisie.

"She has a boyfriend," Felix said.

"Do you mean she's in love?" Great-Uncle Thorne said, his impressively voluminous eyebrows waggling.

"No!" Maisie said.

"Maybe," Felix admitted.

"A peculiar state," Great-Uncle Thorne said, cutting his *croque-monsieur* in the unusual way he always cut things: Fork in his left hand, knife in his right, he cut and took a bite, cut and took a bite, never putting the knife down.

"Can't say that I recommend it," he continued between bites. "Look what it did to my poor, foolish sister."

"Have you ever been in love?" Felix ventured.

"Of course I've been in love," Great-Uncle Thorne bellowed. "But I didn't let it get the best of me like that nitwit sister of mine."

"Who was she?" Felix asked.

"My sister? Why, you nincompoop, your great-aunt Maisie!"

"No, no," Felix said. "Who were you in love with?"

Great-Uncle Thorne's face softened. He put down his fork and knife and stared at some far-off place that neither Felix nor Maisie could see.

"Penelope Merriweather," he said finally. *"Mon amour."* He shook his head and resumed eating.

"What happened to her?" Felix dared to ask.

"Interesting story," Great-Uncle Thorne said. "I assumed she was dead. After all, she'd be ancient by now. But at your great-aunt Maisie's . . ." He faltered for an instant, then cleared his throat and continued. "At her funeral, the Merriweathers' footman handed me a calling card from none other than Penelope herself. Alive and well, after all."

"What's a calling card?" Maisie asked.

"One more lost piece of civilization, my dear niece," Great-Uncle Thorne said, shaking his head sadly. "Everyone used to have them. And your footman would bring your calling card to the person with whom you wished to visit, and they would send their reply back."

"So Penelope Merriweather wanted to visit you?" Felix asked, tickled at the idea of meeting the woman Great-Uncle Thorne had loved.

"Indeed," Great-Uncle Thorne answered.

The clocks in Elm Medona chimed nine o'clock with their various bells, bongs, and tunes.

"In fact," he added with a grin, "she should arrive just about now."

Aiofe, the maid, hurried into the Dining Room, looking quite upset. Her face was flushed, and her eyes were wide.

"Mr. Pickworth," she began. "There's . . . well . . . she . . . I mean . . ."

"Spit it out, you ninny!"

"I . . ."

But Aiofe didn't have to say anything more. A strange shuffling sound came from outside the Dining Room. They all stopped eating to listen as it grew slowly, slowly closer.

Aiofe pointed to the doorway, and everyone turned their gaze there.

After what seemed like forever, a figure appeared.

It took Maisie and Felix a moment to realize it was an actual person standing in front of them. Maybe the tiniest person they'd ever seen. It took another moment for them to realize that the person was a woman. A woman with probably the most wrinkly face in the whole world and a cap of oddly blue curls. She wore glasses that seemed to magnify her eyes a billion times, so that they appeared bright blue and enormous in her tiny face. She was like a bird in so many ways, that if she had actually taken flight, Maisie and Felix would not have been surprised.

By now, Great-Uncle Thorne was on his feet, a look of delight written all over his face.

The woman kept moving toward them, slower than the slowest living thing moved. Her tiny feet, encased in jeweled slippers, shuffled forward. She wore so many bracelets on her thin wrists that her bony arms seemed to be weighed down by them. She positively clanged as she made her way into the Dining Room. She wore a cardboard-brown wool suit, and the jacket had fat bands of black trim along the edges and in slashes across the front, with big gold buttons in the middle.

After what felt like forever, the tiny woman was standing in front of Great-Uncle Thorne.

She tilted her head coquettishly upward.

"Thorne," she said in a strange, girl-like voice.

Great-Uncle Thorne's mouth opened, but no words came out.

"What I was trying to say," Aiofe announced, "is that you have a visitor, Mr. Pickworth."

Aiofe curtsied slightly.

"May I present Miss Penelope Merriweather?"

CHAPTER 4

March Madness

Penelope Merriweather had been a silent movie star, a flapper, a survivor of the *Titanic*.

"That was all so long ago," she said in her funny, childlike voice.

She did not seem sad that she was no longer beautiful. Or that she was—according to Penelope herself—one of the oldest living people in the United States.

"Or is it the world?" Penelope wondered out loud.

Maisie thought it was entirely possible that Penelope Merriweather was indeed the oldest living person in the entire world. Her face had so many crevices and lines that it looked like the topographical map hanging on the back wall of Mrs. Witherspoon's classroom. When Aiofe poured Penelope a cup of coffee in one of the Pickworth china cups, it took her a full minute to get the cup to her lips, and most of the coffee had sloshed out of it by the time it finally reached her mouth.

Penelope's mouth. That was an entire curiosity unto itself. Her lips were so thin that they seemed to hardly be there at all, like the lines of latitude and longitude on the globe that sat in front of the topographical map in Mrs. Witherspoon's classroom. But Penelope wore lipstick—a color that was neither pink nor orange—as if she had regular-size lips.

But despite her decrepitude, her sagging flesh, her glacial movements, Penelope's eyes shone bright and her mind seemed alert and quick.

"Thorne," Penelope said, "you look decades younger than I. What is your secret?"

Maisie and Felix held their breath waiting for Great-Uncle Thorne's answer.

"Well," he replied after a pause, "I send these two back in time, and although I can't explain the physics of it, every time they time travel, I gain back some of my lost vitality."

Maisie and Felix exchanged a look of shock.

Wasn't The Treasure Chest a secret?

Penelope Merriweather blinked several times.

"I don't actually get younger, mind you," Great-Uncle Thorne explained. "I just get, well, healthier."

Penelope's tiny mouth opened as wide as a baby bird's when it's about to be fed, and a girlish giggle let loose.

"That's a good one, Thorne," she gasped.

Great-Uncle Thorne smiled at her. "Isn't it, though?" he said. "Why, before they moved into Elm Medona, I was in a London hospital, deteriorating at an alarming rate. I had no idea they'd been time traveling or I would have understood why I was suddenly healthier and more agile than I'd been in decades."

Maisie gaped at Great-Uncle Thorne. Was that true? she wondered. Had he been in a hospital, like Great-Aunt Maisie?

"Good for you two then," Penelope said good-naturedly. "He looks marvelous."

"You do, too, Penny," Great-Uncle Thorne said in a tone of voice that Maisie and Felix had never heard come out of him before: tender and—could they even use the word?—loving.

"That's true," Penelope said, "if you happen to like pachyderms."

"No, no," Great-Uncle Thorne insisted. "When I look at you I see that beautiful girl I gave my heart to so long ago."

He reached over and took Penelope's liver-spotted hand in his own large, strong one, and squeezed it.

Penelope looked at Maisie and Felix, who by now could do nothing but sit and stare at her and the changes she'd brought on in Great-Uncle Thorne.

"Could you two do some time traveling and work your magic on me?" she asked.

"I regret to have to tell you, Penny, that only Pickworths reap the benefits," Great-Uncle Thorne said. He hadn't let go of her hand, and it rested tucked into his.

"Sounds like Phinneas Pickworth, that scoundrel," she said with a good-natured chuckle. "Of course he would arrange it thus."

"Tell me," Great-Uncle Thorne said, "where do you live these days? I hope it's not in the same dreadful facility where the mother of these two stuck poor Maisie."

Penelope looked surprised. "Why, I live at

Château Glorieux," she said.

Maisie and Felix had passed Château Glorieux on Bellevue Avenue lots of times. It was just as its name suggested: an enormous stone château that looked as if it had been airlifted from somewhere in France and dropped on several hundred acres in Newport.

"But how can you manage?" Great-Uncle Thorne asked.

"Oh," Penelope said with a dismissive wave of her hand, "the staff takes care of everything. I still tend to my roses, of course. I know the Pickworths are peony people, but the Merriweathers have always grown roses."

She turned to Maisie and Felix and added, "The Merriweather Rose is a lovely shade of lavender."

"Quite lovely," Great-Uncle Thorne agreed.

"And I swim in the pool every morning at six," Penelope continued.

Again she turned to Maisie and Felix. "The Merriweathers like saltwater in the pool. And we like it bracingly cold. That's the secret to our longevity."

"Ah! Yes," Great-Uncle Thorne said. "I remember

too well the temperature of the pool at Château Glorieux. There was something about the tiles—"

"Egyptian!" Penelope said. "From the tomb of King Petahu."

She once again faced Maisie and Felix and said, "They tell the story of his life, all along the sides and bottom of the pool. You should come to Château Glorieux for a swim and see for yourself."

"Maybe this summer—" Felix began, just to be polite. Although he loved to swim, he couldn't imagine doing it in March.

Penelope's wrinkly face wrinkled even more in consternation.

"But it's indoors," she said. Then she added, "Of course."

"How about this Saturday?" Great-Uncle Thorne suggested with far too much enthusiasm.

"Saturday, Saturday," Penelope said, thinking. "Yes, I believe Saturday will work."

Slowly, she began to rise from the enormous chair. Great-Uncle Thorne jumped to his feet and offered his arm to steady her.

"Allow me to escort you," he said.

Maisie and Felix stared after them as they made

their way out of the Dining Room.

"She's . . . she's . . . ancient!" Maisie finally blurted.

Felix could only agree.

The sound of Great-Uncle Thorne whistling filled their ears as he returned to the Dining Room. When he walked back inside the room, he stopped, his face positively glowing. He didn't seem to notice Maisie and Felix at all. He just lifted an apple from the crystal bowl of fruit and tossed it into the air, catching it easily.

"Oh, it don't mean a thing if you ain't got your swing," he sang. "Doo-wop, doo-wop, doo . . ."

As soon as Maisie heard her father's voice on the telephone Saturday morning, she said, "I am more miserable than ever."

"Oh, sweetie, that can't be," he said. "Felix said you two are going swimming at some fancy mansion and there's a big party tonight, right?"

"Everyone," Maisie announced dramatically, "is in love."

She expected her father to be alarmed, to question her. But instead, he laughed. "Well, it is spring," he said. Foolishly, she decided.

"Even Great-Uncle Thorne," she added.

Which made her father laugh again. "That's a good one," he said.

"He's in love with the oldest person alive," she said.

Ever since Penelope Merriweather had shuffled into the Dining Room, Great-Uncle Thorne had been acting as stupidly as their mother—looking all dreamy-eyed and saying ridiculous things and being actually nice.

"I thought *he* was the oldest person alive," her father said.

Maisie paused. Her father sounded way too cheerful, she thought.

"Next thing I know," Maisie said, "you're going to tell me you're in love, too."

Her father's voice caught the tiniest bit before he said, again, "It's spring, Maisie."

Maisie felt her heart beating against her ribs. She thought she might throw up.

"Maisie?" her father said.

But she didn't answer. She just held the phone too tight and tried to breathe.

"Felix isn't in love, is he?" her father asked.

"He has Lily Goldberg," Maisie managed to say. Inexplicably, hot tears were splashing down her cheeks. "And . . . and Mom has Bruce Fishbaum," she said, expecting her father to be shocked or outraged, maybe enough to fly here from Qatar and win her mother back.

But instead he said, "I know."

"You know?" Maisie said.

"She told me," he said without even a drop of shock or outrage. "Sweetie, we're divorced. This is what happens when people get divorced."

That's when she knew. Her father was in love, too. With another woman. Without even saying good-bye, Maisie hung up. She sat there staring at the phone as if it had betrayed her. Then she threw up.

"You'd better not come to the party," Felix said hopefully. "You don't want to throw up there."

Felix had never summoned the courage to tell Maisie that she was not invited to Bitsy Beal's March Madness party. And he had not summoned the courage to ask Bitsy Beal if Maisie could come.

Maisie was on her bed with a cool towel on her forehead, her eyes closed and her face pale.

"I'll be okay," she said softly.

Felix said, "I wouldn't risk it."

She opened her eyes and looked at him suspiciously.

"Just saying," he said, shrugging.

Maisie closed her eyes again. "Did Dad mention to you that he has a girlfriend?"

"No," Felix said. "Did he tell you that?"

"Not in so many words."

"Well? What did he say?" Felix asked impatiently. His sister always made him beg for information.

"He said that it's spring."

Exasperated, Felix said, "And from that comment you surmise he has a girlfriend?"

"He knew about Bruce Fishbaum," Maisie said. "And he didn't even care."

"Maisie," Felix said, "don't go jumping to conclusions."

"He said that's what happens when people get divorced."

Felix looked at his sister's pale face. "Is that why you threw up?" he asked her kindly.

She nodded. Tears slid out of the corners of her eyes.

"You'll get tears in your ears from crying on your back," Felix said. That was what their father always used to say if he found one of them crying, and it made Maisie cry harder now.

"We have the worst parents ever," she said.

She looked so pathetic lying there, crying in that ridiculous bed, that Felix knew he had no choice: Maisie was going to come to that party tonight. But, he decided, he didn't have to like it. And she was not going to ruin everything for him.

Great-Uncle Thorne called to Felix as he left Maisie's room.

"Can we have a word?" he asked him. "Man to man?"

"Uh . . . sure," Felix said.

Great-Uncle Thorne grasped Felix by the shoulder. "About our invitation," he began.

"Swimming?"

"Exactly. I'd prefer that you and your sister stay home."

"If you're worried about Maisie throwing up again," Felix explained, "it was just an emotional reaction. She's not sick or anything."

"You see," Great-Uncle Thorne said, as if Felix hadn't spoken, "I would like to be alone with Penelope. You understand."

"Ah," Felix said.

Great-Uncle Thorne gave him a slap on the back and said, "I knew you'd understand. Now I'm off to find my bathing suit. Haven't worn it since the thirties. Or was it the twenties?"

With that, he was off down the hallway, singing, "Oh, it don't mean a thing if you ain't got your swing . . ."

Before Felix could take another step, his mother was calling to him.

"Wanted to say good-bye and happy swimming," she said when she reached him.

"Why are you dressed like that?" Felix asked her, pointing to her belt, which was navy blue and had green whales on it, and then to her brand-new boat shoes, which were a strange shade of red.

"I'm going sailing," she said brightly. "With Bruce."

His mother had on a baseball hat, and her hair, pulled back into a ponytail, popped out the back of it. She was not a person who wore baseball hats.

"Where's your sister?"

"In her room. She threw up."

"Oh, dear. I'd better take her temperature."

Felix shook his head. "She thinks Dad has a girlfriend."

His mother averted her eyes. "Uh-huh."

"Wait. Does Dad have a girlfriend?" Felix asked.

"He has a close female friend, I think, maybe, yes."

"Is that the same as a girlfriend?" Felix demanded.

His mother finally looked up at him. "Yes," she said. "But honey, that's what happens when people get divorced."

"So I've heard," Felix said, feeling weird. In his mind, even though his parents had been divorced for almost a whole year, he still pictured them together somehow. He knew that was dumb, but he couldn't help it. They were his *parents*. They belonged together.

"I guess she's not going to go swimming, then?" his mother said.

"Neither of us are," Felix told her. "Great-Uncle Thorne uninvited us. He wants this to be a date or something."

"A date!"

"Yeah," Felix said, heading to his room to think.

"Apparently everyone is in love around here."

"Well," his mother said brightly, "it is spring, you know."

Bitsy Beal lived in a mansion almost as big as Elm Medona. It had been built in 1898 by Lorne Allan Adrain, a railroad tycoon, and his wife, Zuzu, who was herself extravagantly rich. Zuzu decorated the house with more gold leaf and marble than any other mansion in Newport. Then, bored with it, she had Lorne build her another mansion right next door, and decorated that one entirely in orange, her favorite color. Bitsy's father, who was an oilman from Texas, bought the orange mansion for his first wife in the 1980s and the one next door for his second wife ten years later.

When Maisie learned that, she'd said, "Isn't it totally weird to live next door to your ex-wife?" But now that her own parents were dating other people, she wasn't so sure it was weird after all. Maybe the kids from that first wife were just relieved to have their father nearby, even if it did mean having to live next door to a new wife and Bitsy.

Maisie looked over at the orange mansion while

she and Felix waited for someone to open the door to Bitsy's. Inside that house were Bitsy's stepsisters, who were in high school and had somehow survived their own parents getting divorced and dating and remarrying and even having another kid. She tried not to imagine having Bruce Fishbaum's hockey-star kids as her stepsister and stepbrother, but the thought crept into her brain, anyway, and made her shudder.

"No one is going to understand your costume," Felix told her for the millionth time.

He had on a bright yellow tuxedo jacket and blue bow tie and an oversize green top hat. Maisie was certain just about everybody was going to be the Mad Hatter. But she would be the only one clever enough to dress as one of the March sisters from *Little Women*. She smoothed her long dress, which was also green but a pleasant shade, like moss, and had dozens of tiny buttons down the front. Her shoes also had buttons. She'd found them in the trunk in her closet, too, along with a little hook to button all those buttons.

"They will when I explain it to them," Maisie said. "March Madness."

Felix shook his head, disgusted. He'd been mean

to her all afternoon. If Maisie didn't know better, she would have thought he didn't even want her to come to the party.

As soon as they walked inside, Felix slipped away from Maisie. He made his way through the crowd of kids in the room called the Gold Room because it had more gold leaf than any other room, so much that it absolutely glittered. When he found Lily Goldberg, who was dressed as a tulip, he joined her at the buffet table. It was filled with miniature food: tiny hot dogs in tiny buns, hamburger sliders, little egg rolls, and dumplings.

"You make a very nice tulip," Felix told Lily.

"I know," she said.

He smiled and handed her a glass of lemonade.

"Is that your sister over there?" Lily said, squinting.

Felix followed her gaze across the room to Maisie, who was standing there looking around like she was lost.

"Yes," he muttered.

"What is she wearing?"

"She's a March sister, from—"

"*Little Women!*" Lily said. "That's clever."

"It is?"

"Well, clever but kind of hard to figure out," Lily said. "I mean, she just looks like an old-fashioned person."

"Right," Felix said.

"There's a DJ in the music room," Lily said hopefully.

"Right," Felix said again.

He mustered all the courage he had, then he wiped his hand on his pants to be sure it was good and dry, and then he actually took Lily Goldberg's hand, with its chewed fingernails and small, star-shaped scar at the base of her thumb, in his. To his surprise and utter delight, Lily gave his hand a little squeeze.

Hand in hand, Felix led Lily to the music room.

"What are you supposed to be?" Jim Duncan asked Maisie. "Like, an old lady or something?"

Maisie glared at him. He was wearing basketball shorts, a Duke basketball jersey, and sneakers.

"What are you?" she said. "A basketball player?"

"Well, yeah," he said. "March Madness."

Maisie shrugged. "Whatever."

"March Madness is what they call the NCAA basketball play-offs," Jim explained.

She didn't answer him. She was hot in her long dress and high, buttoned shoes. And she couldn't find Felix to complain to.

"Now you," Jim was saying.

"Jo March," Maisie said.

He looked at her, baffled.

"Forget it," she grumbled.

"No, really, who is he?"

"Do I look like I'm a *he*?" Maisie said, and walked away.

"Joe's a girl?" Jim Duncan called after her.

She wove her way through the crowd, looking for Felix. Almost every boy was dressed as a basketball player and almost every girl was a flower of some kind. Felix had been right. Her costume was all wrong. She should have been a daffodil, an iris, a daisy. When she passed the buffet table, she popped a miniature egg roll into her mouth, then kept walking, following the music that came from another room.

There, a DJ was talking kids through something called the chicken dance. First, they had to flap their arms like wings. Then they moved their hands like two beaks opening and closing. Then more arm flapping before they shook their rear ends like chickens shaking their feathers.

Smack in the middle of the room she spotted Felix chicken-dancing with Lily Goldberg and looking like he was having more fun than he'd ever had before. His face was actually lit up with happiness, and his eyes sparkled as he and Lily shook their butts, grinning at each other.

Felix did not see her standing there looking lonely and miserable. Or if he did, he was pretending he didn't. Maisie went back to the buffet table and ate enough hamburger sliders to add up to one real-size hamburger. Then she didn't know what to do next. The chicken-dance music kept playing, and the sounds of everyone laughing and clucking floated with it through the air. No one else was even in the Gold Room. They were all chicken-dancing.

Maybe his mother was right, Felix thought. Maybe there was something that happened to people in spring. It had happened to Great-Uncle Thorne, and his mother, and his father. And now it was happening to Felix. He had chicken-danced, hokey-pokeyed, hully-gullyed, macarena-ed, and done the Electric Slide, all with Lily Goldberg. She did not leave his side, not once. When Felix smiled at her, she smiled back. In between dances, when Felix took her hand, she held on. He had even forgotten about Maisie in her ridiculous costume. All around him, girls were flowers, dressed in pale leotards and tights—yellow and pink and purple—with felt or fabric petals framing their faces. They looked lovely, these girls. Not at all like Maisie, whose costume smelled a little like mothballs and didn't really make sense.

Yes, Felix forgot that Maisie had come to the party, until the DJ took a break, and Felix and Lily walked hand in hand back to the Gold Room for some more lemonade and miniature snacks.

"Your sister crashed my party," Bitsy Beal said from beneath her daisy crown.

Felix glanced around the room, but Maisie was nowhere in sight.

"Avery said she smelled like an old man's winter coat, and she ate about a million sliders," Bitsy said.

She didn't really expect an answer; Felix saw that. But he gave her one anyway.

"I told her she wasn't invited," he lied. "But she came anyway." He felt weird inside. Weird for lying to appease Bitsy. Weird for betraying Maisie. Untwinning was harder than he thought it would be.

Bitsy shook her head sympathetically. "Poor Felix," she said. "Saddled with a loser."

"She's not a loser," Felix said. "She's just—"

But he couldn't finish. A lump lodged in his throat, and he could hardly swallow, it felt so big. He got another glass of lemonade, hoping that would help it go away. It didn't.

Avery Mason joined them, tossing her beautiful hair.

"Your sister just ran out of here and down Bellevue Avenue," she told Felix. "Barefoot," she added.

Felix had vowed he was not going to let Maisie ruin his night. But why in the world was she barefoot? Running down Bellevue Avenue? He knew he should go after her. Maybe she had heard Bitsy talking about her. Maybe she knew she wasn't invited after all.

The DJ was back, and he put on "The Twist."

Everyone squealed and ran out of the Gold

Room, back to the music room, already starting to dance. This time, Lily took *his* hand. Felix thought about Maisie, practically home by now. Where were her shoes? She had been so amused by them, carefully buttoning each button with that special hook.

"Come on," Lily said, tugging his hand.

Felix pushed away all thoughts about Maisie.

"Time to twist," he said.

They twisted. They spelled out the letters to "YMCA" with their arms. They dropped to the floor for "Shout" and then jumped up high when the song grew loud. They did the limbo, and finally, Felix held Lily by the waist and they danced an awkward, shuffling waltz. And the entire time, that lump stayed in his throat, and no matter how hard he tried not to, Felix thought of Maisie, barefoot, running down Bellevue Avenue alone in the dark.

CHAPTER 5

Buffalo

As soon as Felix got home, he ran through the Foyer, up the Grand Staircase, and down the hall straight to Maisie's room. Elm Medona felt the way it always did at night: too quiet and too creepy. He was relieved to see Maisie's door open and a light on inside.

"Maisie?" Felix said from the doorway. "Maisie, I'm sorry. I'm a terrible brother. I'm an awful person." The words came out in one long, breathless rush.

But Maisie's bed, with mahogany posts elaborately carved into the shapes of different animals—giraffe, zebra, elephant, and jaguar—and the canopy that stretched across the top made of handmade saffron-colored silk, was empty.

Felix stepped into the room and looked around, as if Maisie might pop out of the armoire or come out from under the bed. The mural of a jungle scene that covered the walls glowed in the lamplight.

"Maisie?" he said again, even though it was clear she wasn't there.

She was probably sulking somewhere, Felix thought. Or crying. His stomach twisted with guilt. After he'd heard about Maisie running out of the party, he hadn't really had very much fun. Sure, he'd liked dancing with Lily Goldberg, but the whole time he couldn't stop thinking about his sister.

Felix left Maisie's room and went downstairs to the Library. Empty. He checked the Billiard Room and the Dining Room and then the Kitchen. But Maisie was nowhere to be found. Slowly, Felix made his way up the back stairs from the Kitchen. A terrible thought had lodged in his mind and despite him trying to push it away, it grew bigger and bigger: *What if Maisie never made it home?*

"Maisie?" Felix called into the big, empty house. His throat had gone dry, and his voice came out like a croak.

Should he call his mother? Or the police?

But then a new idea came to Felix. He ran up the Grand Staircase, as fast as he could, and down the hall until he reached the place where, when he pressed it, the wall opened to reveal a secret staircase. His heart pounded as he ran up that staircase. If Maisie wasn't there, he didn't know what he would do.

Felix threw open the door to The Treasure Chest.

And there, to his great relief, was Maisie.

"Why didn't you tell me I wasn't invited to the party?" Maisie asked Felix.

To his surprise, she didn't sound angry. Instead, her voice came out flat and emotionless.

"I don't know," he said. "I guess I didn't want you to feel bad."

She nodded. She was sitting on the floor with objects all around her: a tortoise shell and an animal skull; a test tube and a small, jeweled crown; a crystal, a wooden block, a long red-tailed hawk feather.

"You figured I wouldn't feel humiliated putting on a costume and going to a party where no one even talked to me," she said.

"Jim Duncan talked to you," Felix said helplessly.

Maisie nodded again. "You figured," she continued in that strange, flat voice, "that I wouldn't hear everybody making fun of me."

"I . . ." Felix began, but he stopped, because what could he say?

Maisie picked up the feather. "It really doesn't work alone," she said. "I've been up here trying."

"You know it doesn't," Felix said, sitting on the floor beside her. The animal skull was whitewashed and creepy.

"I know," she said.

"I'm sorry," Felix said, but it sounded weak, not genuine.

Maisie was still dressed in her old-fashioned outfit, but Felix saw that she had different shoes on now. Not the high, buttoned ones she'd worn to the party, but her lime-green sneakers with the mismatched laces. Those laces *were* ironic, he decided. Why had he been such a jerk to her about them?

"Phinneas must have been some kind of weirdo," Maisie said. "I mean, making an anagram from something in a French novel about time travel. Like he was practically telling the whole world."

"Maybe Great-Uncle Thorne has something to say about it," Felix offered, hoping Maisie might agree and leave The Treasure Chest with him to find Thorne and ask him. Hoping her voice would go back to normal.

"He's having a late supper with Penelope Merriweather," Maisie said. "And Mom is out with her *boyfriend*. And you've been with Lily Goldberg. It's just been me and all of Phinneas's collection. Because I guess I got my weird genes from him."

"You're not—"

"Oh, please," Maisie said.

Usually when Maisie got angry with him, she ignored him. She cried. This was different, like she was beyond angry. Felix tried to think of how to make it up to her.

But before he came up with an idea, Maisie looked straight at him, her eyes steely. She held out the red-tailed hawk feather she was holding.

"You owe me," she said.

She was right. He owed her big-time. Felix reached out and held the soft tip of the feather, and immediately he and Maisie were lifted from the floor, tumbling through time.

When Maisie landed, she opened her eyes and saw that she was staring up at an enormous, hairy, smelly animal. It stared back at her. It had big brown eyes with a long fringe of eyelashes around them. Although it was dark out, the full moon and a sky full of twinkling stars lit the night.

Maisie blinked.

She blinked again.

"Buffalo," she said softly.

As soon as she said it, she realized that she wasn't exactly seeing one buffalo. She was smack in the middle of hundreds of them. All around her, as far as she could see. Buffalo.

Slowly, Maisie got to her feet, trying to decide if buffalo were the type of animal that might charge a person, like bulls or moose. The air smelled like the monkey house at the Bronx Zoo, except worse. As hard as she tried to think, Maisie realized that she knew absolutely nothing about the temperament of buffalo.

She looked around for Felix, but he was nowhere in sight. Or at least, nowhere that she could see past the herd of shaggy beasts that surrounded her.

Maisie carefully made her way through the animals, squeezing in between them. The heat from their bodies, and her fear that at any moment they might decide to do something other than just stand there, made her sweat. One thing she knew for sure: A herd of buffalo sure did stink.

When Felix landed, he hit something hard and hairy, then fell from its great height, hard onto the grass. He looked down the full height of the thing, which was not at all happy about having a twelve-year-old boy drop out of nowhere onto its back. He had seen enough movies to know he was looking at a buffalo. An angry buffalo. The animal snorted and pawed the ground with its hooves. It dipped its head and snorted some more.

Felix rolled out of the way, right into another buffalo. In fact, there were buffalo as far as he could see. Hundreds of them. Maybe thousands.

"Sorry," he said to the snorting one in front of him.

His voice sounded small in the vast night.

The buffalo pawed at the grass again, its hooves so close that Felix could see the bits of grass and dirt stuck in them. If this buffalo charged, the whole herd might follow suit, he thought. But if Felix ran, would it follow him and start a stampede? Did buffalo stampede? Or was that just horses?

Felix got to his knees, carefully backing away from the buffalo and trying to avoid any of the other ones. They were standing pretty much shoulder to shoulder, which made it hard to maneuver. Felix couldn't believe that just a couple of hours ago he'd been happily dancing the chicken dance with Lily Goldberg. Now here he was in the middle of a herd of buffalo, in the middle of who knows where, scared that he was about to get gored or crushed. He struggled to his feet. The buffalo nearest him shifted, trapping him between it and another one. Felix held his breath until the buffalo shifted again, and then he managed to get free. Luckily, he'd lost sight of the angry one, but now he was lost in a sea of buffalo, trying his best to get out of the herd.

Once again a buffalo shifted, this time trapping Felix between its haunches and the haunches of another one. Their tails swished lazily. They didn't seem like they were about to move again.

Felix placed his hands on the animal's hairy back

and tried to push it away. But when it turned its large head toward him—unhappily, Felix thought—Felix stopped. Instead, he wiggled his body until, inch by inch, he worked his way out and smacked into something very un-buffalo-like.

He screamed and turned, afraid of what he might see next.

And there was Maisie, turning to look at him over her shoulder.

"Buffalo," she whispered.

"No kidding," Felix said.

"We just have to make it over there," she said, pointing her chin.

"Oh," he said, "is that all?" There were about a zillion buffalo between them and over there.

"Slow and steady," she said.

Felix took her hand and did what she suggested. Together they made their slow, steady way through the herd.

"They're kind of cute," Maisie said from the grass where they sat beyond the buffalo.

"If they're not going to kill you, sure," Felix said.

He scanned the horizon. It appeared they really

were in the middle of nowhere. Felix saw nothing but buffalo and grass stretching seemingly forever.

Maisie lay down, putting her head on her arms.

"In the morning we'll be able to figure out where we are," she said.

"I hope so," Felix said.

He touched the feather in his yellow tuxedo jacket pocket. One thing he knew for certain: There had not been this many buffalo in a long time. They were practically extinct. Another thing he knew— they had roamed the western states. Felix sighed and tried to stop thinking about it. Maisie was right. Once morning came, they would be able to figure out where to go and what to do. He closed his eyes and listened to the sound of absolute silence until he finally fell asleep.

Maisie wasn't sure what woke her up, the sound of horses pounding toward them or the strange shrieking. Whichever it was, Maisie and Felix startled awake at the same time, jumping to their feet. For a second, they saw nothing but the buffalo, which looked even bigger in the early morning light.

Then, across the prairie came dozens of Native Americans on horses, bows and arrows lifted. They were shirtless, with rawhide quivers of arrows slung over their bare shoulders. Their hair was long and black and flew in the breeze. Felix saw that they wore feathers in it. He once again reached into his pocket and touched the red-tailed hawk feather from The Treasure Chest. Maisie had been right. Things were clear now. One of these Native Americans needed this feather. But how would they ever figure out which one?

He didn't have time to consider any longer. The buffalo, which had seemed temporarily frozen, suddenly began to run, their big brown bodies kicking up clouds of dust.

One of the men gave a long, loud call, and almost in unison, arrows flew. One. Two. Three.

Another call.

And it was over.

The dust seemed to float in the air for a moment before it settled, revealing the dead bodies of buffalo as far as Maisie and Felix could see.

Maisie swallowed hard, her hand reaching out to find her brother's. The stink of blood and musk made her want to throw up. She gulped again, holding on tight to Felix's hand.

Across the plains, a sea of Native Americans descended on the dead buffalo. As Felix watched them, he realized where he and Maisie had landed. They were in the American West. And white settlers were the enemy.

"Maisie," he whispered hoarsely. "We've got to get out of here before they see us."

At first, she looked puzzled, but slowly she understood what Felix meant.

Her eyes scanned the endless stretch of land around them. There was no place to run without being seen.

"Uh-oh," Maisie muttered.

Felix squinted. Here and there he saw large rocks or clumps of sagebrush. Maybe they could dash from one to the other, crouching until it was safe to continue on. But before he could tell Maisie his plan, a hand landed on his shoulder and held on to him hard. Another hand landed on Maisie's, keeping her in place, too.

Maisie and Felix both turned to find a girl about their age glaring at them. Her dark hair fell to her shoulders in two braids, and she wore a brown dress made of animal hides. Beneath the fringed hem, Maisie glimpsed brown pants, also made of hides. Even when their eyes met, the girl did not let go.

"We . . ." Felix began, but then he stopped. How could he possibly explain why he and Maisie were standing here?

The girl studied them with great seriousness. After what seemed forever, she released Maisie and lifted her finger to her lips.

"Sshh," she said softly.

With her other hand, she motioned for them to follow her.

"Is she taking us prisoner?" Maisie managed to ask.

But Felix could only shrug and follow the girl's moccasins as she lightly skipped across the grass.

After a very long time, a village of tepees appeared on the horizon. The girl had not said a word to Maisie and Felix or slowed down to wait for them when they lagged behind. But as they neared the village, she finally stopped.

"Cheyenne," the girl said, pointing to the tepees.

"My people."

Felix nodded.

The girl pointed to herself. "Yellow Feather," she said.

"Felix," Felix said, tapping his chest.

Yellow Feather laughed. "Fe. Licks," she repeated.

"Maisie," Maisie said.

"Maize?" Yellow Feather asked.

"Well, Maisie."

"Hmph," Yellow Feather said, and motioned for them to follow.

"Maize is corn," Felix told Maisie, grinning. "She thinks you're named after corn for some reason."

"I know what maize is," Maisie grumbled.

Now she could see that the tepees were enormous hides wrapped around tall wooden poles, painted brightly with scenes of buffalo hunts or men on horseback fighting with bows and arrows. Smoke rose from the center of the village, and the smell of meat cooking reminded Maisie that she hadn't eaten since Bitsy Beal's party the night before.

Yellow Feather pointed again, this time to the men returning with the buffalo. Horses thundered across the plains in the distance.

"No girls allowed to hunt," Yellow Feather said angrily.

She put her hands on her hips and watched, scowling, as the men grew closer.

"Only men," she added.

Felix caught up with Maisie and Yellow Feather.

"Will you eat all that buffalo meat?" he asked as he took in the sight of all the dead animals the men were bringing into the village.

Yellow Feather looked at him as if he had just said the most ridiculous thing she'd ever heard. Once again she motioned for Maisie and Felix to follow her. This time she led them to a tepee where one of the dead buffalo had already been deposited.

She kneeled beside it and gently touched its stomach.

"Pot to cook in," she said. "Or to carry water."

Yellow Feather ran her hands along its hair. "Rope," she said. "And belts. And beneath," she added, pointing to the ribs, "we make sleds from these."

Then she touched the strong muscles on its back. She held up an imaginary bow. "Strong," she said, and Maisie and Felix both nodded, understanding that somehow the muscle could be used to make the string of the bow.

"And this," Yellow Feather continued, miming sewing.

"Thread," Felix said.

"Yes," Yellow Feather said. "Thread."

She lifted the animal's leg and pointed to its bone there. Once again she mimed sewing.

"A needle?" Maisie offered.

"Needle," Yellow Feather said, nodding. "And used as tools. And to paint our clothes and tepees."

Still on her knees, she moved up to the buffalo's head. It was hard for Felix to still watch with the buffalo's tongue jutting out and its eyes glazed and staring back at him. But Yellow Feather grew even more animated, and he forced himself to pay attention to her.

"Very special," she said solemnly as she poked the purple tongue. "For ceremony."

Maisie nodded, even though she was only watching out of the corner of her eye.

Now Yellow Feather knocked on the horns. She mimicked eating and drinking.

"Spoons," Maisie said.

"Cups," Felix added.

Yellow Feather beamed up at them. She scurried down to the other end of the buffalo. Relieved to not have to look at its face anymore, Felix and Maisie followed her. She lifted something dried on its back legs.

"Make fire," she said.

Maisie scrunched up her face. "That's poop," she whispered to Felix.

"Most important," Yellow Feather was saying. "Hides. For tepees. For blankets. For clothes. For drums. For food."

She got to her feet, looking angry again.

"You waste buffalo," she said, pointing now at Maisie and Felix.

"No, no," Felix said quickly. "We recycle everything."

Yellow Feather frowned at him.

"We don't even hunt buffalo where we come from," Maisie said.

Yellow Feather considered this.

"You come from Washington, DC?" she asked finally.

"Near there," Felix said. "No buffalo."

"I don't trust white settlers," she said. "But we always share our food, our tepee." She seemed to be deciding what she should do.

Felix tried to think of what to say. The truth was, she shouldn't trust them. He knew the white settlers were going to take her land and kill off the buffalo. But he wanted her to trust *him*.

"We're friends," Maisie said.

Yellow Feather looked hard at Maisie, and then at Felix.

Felix nodded eagerly. "Friends," he repeated.

"Come to tepee," she ordered.

They had no choice but to follow her.

"Let's give her the feather and get out of here," Maisie whispered.

For once, Felix agreed right away.

CHAPTER 6

Attacked!

"Do not want that," Yellow Feather said, pushing the feather away.

"But you have to take it," Felix said, thrusting it toward her again.

Yellow Feather shook her head. "No," she said.

Felix looked at Maisie helplessly.

"I guess she's not the right one," Maisie said.

"But she's the only person we've seen," Felix said. "Except for all of them." He pointed his chin toward the hunters.

"Mother," Yellow Feather said as a woman approached the tepee.

The two spoke in Cheyenne, glancing at Maisie and Felix from time to time. Finally, Yellow Feather said, "You eat. You stay in tepee."

"Okay," Maisie said, certain that they were in the wrong place. They needed to leave and find the right person to give the feather to.

Yellow Feather's mother motioned for them to come with her, and together they walked to the center of the village, where food was being prepared.

A big fire roared and hissed as meat cooked on it. A rawhide blanket laid on the ground had bowls of berries, cherries, and small, wrinkled plums. Families were gathered there. Children ran around, chasing each other. Many of the women had babies asleep in papooses on their backs. The men were unloading the dead buffalo, leaving the women to prepare the meal and take care of the children.

Yellow Feather pointed to the meat.

"Buffalo," she told Maisie and Felix.

Felix was going to just eat the fruit and berries. But Maisie thought it smelled delicious.

When the men joined everyone, Yellow Feather's mother spoke to them. They all listened as she talked, but their eyes stayed on Maisie and Felix. One man stepped forward and studied them carefully. The chief, perhaps. All of the men wore feathers in their hair, but this one had a full headdress of them. He lifted Felix's chin and looked directly into his eyes, then did the same to Maisie. Felix felt himself trembling beneath the chief's gaze. Surely he was deciding whether they would live or die, Felix thought.

The chief said something to Maisie and Felix, but they couldn't understand.

"He will let you eat with us," Yellow Feather translated.

"Thank you," they both said.

With that, the silence ended and a celebration began. Plates of buffalo meat were passed around, and everyone took berries and fruit.

"This is good," Maisie said to Felix, her mouth full.

"No, thank you," he said, biting into a little plum.

The sun began to set, turning the sky deep orange and red. Yellow Feather invited Maisie and Felix to sit beside her to watch the men give a dance in thanks for the successful hunt.

"They are thanking Wakan Tanka," Yellow Feather explained. "The Great Mystery. It bring buffalo."

The men danced around the fire, chanting in

unison, their bodies covered in paint and buffalo skins draped over their backs.

A chill settled over the village, but Maisie and Felix became so entranced by the ceremony that they hardly noticed. The men danced well into the night. When they finished, the fire had burned down to just orange embers glowing in the darkness, and above them the sky twinkled with more stars than either Felix or Maisie could remember ever seeing. An animal howled in the distance, but otherwise silence fell over everything.

"Maisie," Felix whispered. "I'm sorry."

"I know," she said, because she did know he was sorry. But she could not find the words to explain to him how bad she felt, how utterly alone and alienated she was.

Yellow Feather's voice interrupted.

"Come now," she said. "Sleep."

The tepees were arranged in a circle around the fire. Yellow Feather led them to one, lifting the flap for them to enter. It took a few minutes for Maisie's eyes to get used to the dark, but then she saw that the tepee floor was lined with buffalo hides. *Like wall-to-wall carpeting,* she thought. Already Yellow

Feather's parents lay under buffalo-skin blankets on the left side of the tepee. Maisie could make out other vague shapes beneath blankets, too.

"Sisters," Yellow Feather said.

She indicated two other blankets on the empty right side of the tepee.

"Sleep," she said through a yawn.

"Thank you," Felix told Yellow Feather.

But she had already slipped away.

He and Maisie burrowed under the blankets. Felix tried to sleep, but he couldn't get the images of all that he'd seen that day out of his head. The buffalo hunt. Yellow Feather showing them how all the parts of the buffalo were used. The meat roasting on the open fire. The men thanking Wakan Tanka, their chanting and dancing. The silence. The smells of smoke and meat and sweat. He opened his eyes, and through the triangle opening at the top of the tepee he saw the Big Dipper, right overhead. In his mind, Felix imagined the other constellations and where they were in the night sky, until finally, with Maisie breathing deeply beside him, he, too, fell asleep.

"Much work," Yellow Feather said.

Maisie and Felix struggled awake to find Yellow Feather looming over them, slapping her palms together.

"Buffalo," she said.

"Now what?" Maisie grumbled as she stepped out into the early morning sun.

Yellow Feather handed them each a long, dry strip of buffalo jerky, then told them to follow her.

"Tastes like Slim Jims," Maisie told Felix, who was sniffing at it.

"I never liked Slim Jims," he reminded her. The thought of those slimy, cellophane-wrapped sticks made his stomach lurch.

"But better," Maisie added.

Felix smiled at his sister gratefully. No one in the world knew him better than she did, and thinking that made his heart tumble. He had been such a jerk to her, he thought, vowing to make it up to her somehow when they got back to Newport.

He stuck the jerky into his yellow tuxedo jacket pocket and was glad he hadn't tasted it when he saw what lay ahead.

The women of the tribe were all cutting apart the buffalo from yesterday's hunt. The smell of raw meat was sickening. Felix tried not to notice the flies buzzing around them, or the way the women sliced the red meat into long strips, or the row of buffalo tongues on the ground in front of him.

"Buffalo," Yellow Feather said with a smile, and she picked up a knife and set to work separating meat from skin.

"I guess we should help?" Maisie said.

"Gee," Felix said hopefully, "there aren't any boys here. Maybe this is women's work."

"No way are you leaving me here to skin a buffalo," Maisie told him.

Felix sighed. If he was going to make it up to her, he had to stay.

Reluctantly, he watched as Yellow Feather worked, trying to learn how she was able to cut the meat like that.

By the time mid-morning arrived, both Maisie and Felix were able to cut the buffalo meat into the long strips that would be dried in the sun for jerky. The work had a rhythm to it that made time pass pleasantly. After a while, Maisie and Felix almost forgot the nature of what they were doing and instead lost themselves in the lilting sound of the women's voices and the way in which everyone worked equally. They felt proud of the meat they cut and happy to be able to contribute to the tribe.

Perhaps that was why they didn't hear the sounds of horses approaching.

When the soldiers came thundering into the village, everyone was caught by surprise. Six hundred soldiers dressed in blue uniforms attacked the village on horseback.

One minute, Felix was sitting under the warm sun, surrounded by women and buffalo meat. The next, bullets were flying overhead and pandemonium erupted.

Maisie immediately understood.

"They're attacking us!" she shouted, ducking.

Felix stood up, watching in disbelief as around him, bodies began to fall. He thought of the buffalo hunt yesterday, how the animals had dropped so quickly right in front of him. But these weren't buffalo. These were the people of the tribe who had taken him and Maisie in.

Maisie yanked him down to the ground.

"Stay down," she hissed.

She began to crawl on her stomach toward one of

the nearby tepees. Unsure what else to do, Felix did the same.

By the time they reached the tepee, the shooting had stopped. In its place came the sounds of moans and screams. Maisie and Felix crawled inside the tepee and closed the flaps tight before breaking into frightened sobs.

"Why would they attack like that?" Maisie finally managed to ask.

But Felix couldn't answer.

"It was a massacre," Maisie said. "No one had any weapons to fight back."

Felix put his arm around his sister. The two of them sat like that, afraid to go out, afraid of what they might see or who might be waiting.

But in no time, the smell of smoke became so strong that Felix had to open the flap and look outside.

The soldiers were still there.

He watched as they rode through the village with torches, setting tepees on fire as they rode past them.

They were heading toward where he and Maisie sat.

Roughly, he grabbed his sister's arm and pulled

her out of the tepee, rolling away from it.

They had hardly escaped before that tepee, too, ignited.

By now, the entire village was ablaze. Maisie and Felix sat helplessly as all around them, everything burned.

Neither of them could say how much time passed before a shadow fell over them. Maisie and Felix sat motionless, huddled together, each lost in their own thoughts about the horror that had unfolded before them. But both of them wondered if their friend Yellow Feather had been killed. The thought was too awful to say out loud.

They looked up when the shadow appeared. A boy of fourteen or fifteen stood staring down at them. Although his skin was quite light and his hair almost dirty blond, they could tell he was Native American by his sharp features and clothing made from animal hides. He was not very tall, but he was muscular, and his light-brown eyes bore into them as he loomed above them.

It took them a moment before they realized that Yellow Feather stood behind him, her cheeks streaked with tears. She had a gash on her forehead and another at her temple.

"Mad Bear," Yellow Feather said, as if that explained everything.

"Mad bear?" Felix repeated.

"Soldier," Yellow Feather said, nodding.

Two more Native American boys joined them. They stared down angrily at Maisie and Felix.

"My village," one of them said, and he swept his arms wide. "Destroyed."

"Why?" Maisie cried.

"Revenge," the light-skinned one said. "Grattan defeated near Fort Laramie last year, and Mad Bear cannot forget."

He spit in the dirt before continuing.

"Army stupid," he said. "This camp did not have anything to do with Grattan. Those people long gone. But they kill ninety innocent Lakota today."

He shook his head.

"To you," he said, his eyes on Maisie and Felix, "we are all alike."

"No!" Felix said. "Not at all."

But the boy was already turning from them.

One of the others spoke to him in quiet tones.

Yellow Feather joined in to speak for the twins.

Finally, reluctantly, he turned back to Maisie and Felix.

"Little Thunder and Yellow Feather insist I take you along," he said, without even a hint of warmth in his voice.

"Thank you," Felix said quickly.

"I don't like the white settlers," he said evenly.

"Uh-huh," Felix said.

"They don't understand us," he said.

Felix tried to think of what to say, but the boy was climbing onto his horse already.

"They call him Curly," Yellow Feather said.

Curly did not sound like a very scary name, but this boy was frightening, Maisie thought.

"His hair," Yellow Feather added.

"Where is he taking us?" Maisie asked as two other boys arrived leading horses.

Curly himself answered.

"The Black Hills," he said. "To my people."

CHAPTER 7

Touching the Enemy

Among many other things that she considered on that long, hot day sitting behind Curly on a horse, Maisie wished she had paid more attention to the US geography unit in school last month. Every day, Mrs. Witherspoon had handed out xeroxed maps of different sections of the country, starting with New England and moving to the Mid-Atlantic states, the South, the Midwest, all the way to the Pacific Northwest. And somewhere on one of those xeroxed maps were the Great Plains states. To Maisie, they had looked like Legos, a series of big squares or rectangles, indistinguishable from one another. Now she was moving across those squares and rectangles toward the Black Hills, a place she vaguely remembered Mrs. Witherspoon talking about. But what had she said about them? And where were they exactly?

Maisie sighed and shifted her weight. She'd had no idea how sore a person got riding a horse for all these hours. And Curly apparently was not a believer in stopping to take a break. Her father always stopped when they took family trips. He stopped for coffee and French fries and to read roadside signs and historical markers. He stopped to stretch his legs. Her mother, on the other hand, never stopped. "Why dillydally?" she would say. "Let's just get there already." "The journey is half the fun," her father always answered philosophically. Maybe a difference like that was one of the reasons they got divorced. Maybe a person who enjoys the journey shouldn't marry a person in a hurry. Maisie sighed again. She was a person who liked to take a break, she decided.

As if he'd read her mind, Curly suddenly stopped.

"Horses need water," he announced.

"People need water," Maisie muttered.

He gave her that look of his that told her he did not like her, not one bit. Then he led the horse down a small embankment to a river.

"Um, could you help me off?" Maisie asked him, peering down the great height of the chestnut-brown horse.

Curly scowled but offered his hand. She landed with a thud.

"Thanks," she said, hoping he caught the sarcasm in her voice.

Maisie dusted herself off and watched as the others appeared over the hill. She was happy to see Felix, who looked as miserable as she felt, sitting behind Little Thunder.

"My rear end is killing me," Felix whispered to her when he finally got off the horse.

"I know," Maisie said. "How far do you think the Black Hills are, anyway?"

Felix shrugged. "They're in South Dakota," he said, as if that meant something.

Of course he'd paid attention to the US geography unit. His teacher, Miss Landers, at least made things interesting. Each student in his class got assigned a state, and they had to give an oral report and make a visual representation of it. Felix's state was Alabama, and he'd used the state nut—the pecan—to create its shape. He'd loved his project, loved presenting all the facts about Alabama: state flower, the camellia; state tree, the southern longleaf pine; state fruit, the blackberry; state capital, Montgomery. He'd played the song "Angel from Montgomery" on a continuous loop in the background. It was one of his father's favorite songs, one that he played a lot in those days after they'd told Felix and Maisie about the divorce, before he actually moved out.

Felix tried not to think about that now. No divorce. No Alabama. In fact, what he wished was that his state project had been on South Dakota, because then he might have some idea about where they were going and when they might get there.

"South Dakota," Maisie was saying. "The Black Hills."

"I think the capital is Pierre," Felix said hopefully. "But it's not pronounced the way it's spelled, like the French boy's name. It's pronounced like *peer*."

He could picture Avery Mason giving the report on South Dakota, her beautiful hair glistening as she made the class repeat after her: *peer*.

"I don't think it's even a state yet," Maisie said. "We must be in 18 . . . what? Fifty-something?"

"Alabama became a state in 1819," Felix said.

"Big deal! We're not in Alabama!" Maisie said, frustrated.

"I know, I know," Felix said.

"The square states didn't become states until the late 1800s," she said. "Right?"

"Right."

He tried to remember what else Avery Mason had said in her report.

"I think the state flower is a pasqueflower," Felix said, suddenly remembering Avery Mason making them repeat that after her, too. "It's like a buttercup," he added.

"Great," Maisie said. "I'll be sure to look out for pasqueflowers while I'm there."

Little Thunder passed a cup of water to Felix. As thirsty as he was, he couldn't help but think about how that cup had been made from a buffalo's horn. He squeezed his eyes shut and forced himself to take a sip. Relieved that it tasted like water and not at all like horn, Felix took another big swallow before handing it to Maisie.

Too soon, they were back on the horses, their arms wrapped around the boys' waists, galloping across the Great Plains.

To Maisie, the ride across the Great Plains was about the dullest thing she could remember doing. The landscape was just grass and grass and more grass. Sometimes she would glimpse a herd of buffalo in the distance or see the smoke rising from a village of tepees. But those sights did nothing to alleviate her boredom.

Felix, however, grew to think the plains were quite beautiful. The sky seemed bigger out here. And closer, as if he could reach out and actually touch it. The blue was bluer than back home, a dramatic, breathtaking blue that he had never seen before. The way the sky met the grass seemed almost unreal, like he was living in a giant painting. Late in the afternoon, he watched as storm clouds gathered. Gray and tumultuous, they rolled across the sky toward Felix and the small party of travelers. Lightning split through the clouds and met the ground somewhere far off.

When the rain finally reached them, Felix found it uplifting. He had watched the storm gather itself and move across the sky. He lifted his face and let the rain fall on him. It was his rain, he thought. He'd observed it as it developed and seen it coming toward him.

Soon, though, the rain stopped, and they were now on the horizon hills of craggy rocks loomed.

Felix wondered how Curly knew where to find his tribe. But he had no chance to ask him. In no time they were stopping at a village of tepees, and a man was running out of one to meet them.

"Father of Curly," Little Thunder explained. "Worm."

By the time they had gotten off their horses, Worm had arrived. He listened as Curly described in Lakota what had happened to Little Thunder's village. His eyes were gentle as he studied Maisie and Felix, nodding as his son spoke.

"Worm is not a warrior," Little Thunder told them. "He's a shaman."

"A what?" Maisie asked.

"An interpreter of dreams," Little Thunder said. "And a healer."

Curly had finally gone silent. He led the horses away, but Worm stayed put.

"Welcome," he said to Maisie and Felix.

The fear that both of them had felt since the

attack that morning began to melt away in his presence.

"You are from the Holy Road?" he asked them.

Maisie shook her head no.

"No?" he said, surprised. "White settlers are growing in numbers there."

He didn't wait for them to say anything more but rather motioned for them to follow him into the village.

"You are lucky," Little Thunder said. "The Lakota are tolerant people."

The familiar smell of roasting buffalo meat greeted them. This time, Felix eagerly took some when one of the women offered it to him. He was hungry. He was tired. But mostly, he was safe.

"Psssst," Curly hissed into Felix's ear the next morning. "You come into battle with me."

Felix's eyes opened.

"Battle?" he said.

Images of the bullets flying overhead yesterday flooded his mind, followed by the bows and arrows shot the day before during the buffalo hunt.

"I don't think so," he added.

"You come with me," Curly said. "Touch the enemy."

"Really," Felix said as Curly pulled him out from beneath the buffalo blanket, "I don't want to touch anybody."

Curly studied him a moment, then nodded. He went over to the other side of the tepee, and returned with buckskin leggings and a pair of moccasins.

"For battle," he said, handing them to Felix.

He stood, waiting.

Reluctantly, Felix traded his yellow tuxedo jacket, black pants, and white shirt for the clothes Curly had given him.

"What's going on?" Maisie asked sleepily.

"He wants me to go into battle," Felix said, his voice trembling.

"Touch enemy," Curly told Maisie.

"What enemy?" Maisie asked him.

"Comanche," Curly said.

"Are you going to scalp them?" Maisie asked, sitting up now.

Curly kneeled beside her and made a circle with his hands.

"Scalps round, like the sun," he said softly.

"Powerful, like the sun. We take scalp, we get power."

"I . . . I don't want to take anybody's scalp," Felix said.

Curly laughed. "Only take scalp of dead man," he said. "We touch enemy."

"You keep saying that," Felix said, shivering without his shirt on. "What do you mean exactly?"

"More brave to touch enemy than to kill him," Curly said as he got to his feet.

"It is?" Felix asked, unsure whether he should be relieved or not at this information.

"Shoot bow and arrow from very far away," Curly said. "To touch enemy, you must be very close."

Felix was definitely not relieved.

From outside came the sound of voices and horses.

"Time to go," Curly said, slapping Felix on the back. "Time to count coup. Brave things that you do," he added. "Coup. Every time you touch enemy, you get one coup."

Felix looked at Maisie for some help, but she was jumping up, excited.

"I want to touch the enemy," she said. "I want to count coup."

Curly laughed again. "Girls do not go to battle," he said. "You stay here."

"But I want to come," Maisie insisted. "I'm braver than him." She pointed at Felix.

"We shall see how brave he is," Curly said, his eyes twinkling.

The plan was to surprise the Comanche.

Felix tried to listen hard as Curly explained the way they would ride up on them from over the hill, how the first one to touch a Comanche with his coup stick was the bravest warrior.

"Remember," he told Felix, "only three other men can touch same enemy."

"I really don't think I'll be touching anyone," Felix said, but Curly was already moving away from him.

"Actually," Felix called to Curly's back, "I don't really feel comfortable on this horse by myself."

It was no use.

Everyone was ready, and Felix could not figure out a way to stay behind. He considered just turning around and hightailing it out of there, but by now he was surrounded by excited, eager, bare-chested guys on horseback. Most of them had feathers in their long hair, and they all swung their coup sticks in the air. At least they wouldn't be shooting bows and arrows, he thought. But then a worse idea hit him. The Lakota weren't going to use bows and arrows. But that didn't mean the Comanche weren't.

Alone in the tepee, Maisie took the long red-tailed hawk feather from her pocket. She supposed they were meant to give it to Curly. If she was right, once they did that, they would go back to Newport. For Maisie, back to being a social outcast. At least here Felix was forced to be with her. At home he would get swallowed up by his friends. Everyone at Anne Hutchinson Elementary School would continue adoring him for his skills on the baseball field and his role as class president. All the while, Maisie would stay invisible, unnoticed, ignored.

What if I just hide the feather for a little while? she wondered. Maybe she could have a real talk with Felix about how she felt. She didn't think she could convince him that Bitsy Beal and her crew were shallow and mean, but she might be able to remind him that his loyalties belonged with her, not them. Weren't they twins, after all? Before they were born, they'd curled around each other, heartbeat to heartbeat. Their mother had a sonogram picture of them holding hands in the womb, first and only best friends.

Maisie's eyes darted around the tepee. There was no place to really hide anything. And the Lakota did not have many belongings. But then she saw a small rawhide bag hanging from one of the poles. It had long fringe at the bottom, and a diamond pattern painted across it.

She took it down from the pole and opened the drawstrings at the top. Inside she found an elaborately carved pipe; two large, yellowed animal teeth; and a brown-and-white feather.

"Perfect," Maisie said out loud, tucking the red-tailed hawk feather into the bag with the other things and returning it to its spot on the pole.

No one would look in there for anything, she thought, satisfied. And when the time came, she would take the red-tailed hawk feather out, give it to Curly, and go home.

Felix and his horse were swept up in the movement of the other horses, racing across the grasslands, beneath the white stone hills. They moved as if they were one unit. No one slowed or paused, but rather everyone surged forward. Clouds of dust, kicked up by the horses, filled Felix's eyes and nose, blurring his vision. With his eyes tearing and his nose running, they moved down a hill and then came surging up the other side, into a group of surprised Comanche.

Almost immediately, Curly touched one of them with his coup stick, causing a roar of excitement to rise among the Lakota. Inspired, they moved through the Comanche, coup sticks flying.

Frightened, Felix watched the looks of surprise on the faces of those who got touched, followed by cries of anger. He knew he was expected to do something, to raise his stick and move toward the enemy. But he was too scared to even try.

Just then, a Comanche on horseback came face-to-face with Felix, his black eyes blazing.

He shouted something that Felix could not understand.

Felix lifted his hands in surrender, the way people did in the movies.

But apparently that was not a universal signal.

As he lifted his hands, the Comanche raised his bow and easily pulled an arrow from the rawhide quiver slung over his shoulder.

"Wait!" Felix said. "This means I give up!"

He waved his hands frantically.

The Comanche's gaze did not waver from Felix, even as he slid an arrow into the bow.

He was so close that Felix could easily make out the glint of the sharp point and see the feathers on the other end.

Suddenly, he remembered his coup stick, which dangled limply from his hand. With every bit of energy he could muster, he lifted it and touched the Comanche on the arm.

Felix's heart pounded with a mix of terror and pride. He pressed his knees hard into the horse, sending it galloping forward and away. It took Felix a moment to realize the loud cry of triumph he heard was actually coming from him.

The sound of hooves pounding up beside him made him glance over to find Curly, sitting tall on his own horse, grinning.

"White boy made first coup," Curly said, impressed.

"I did?" Felix asked.

"Highest honor," Curly said.

They held each other's gaze long enough to acknowledge Curly's newfound respect for Felix.

Then, urging his horse to go even faster, Felix bent low and held on to its neck as the wind whistled around him.

First coup, he thought. *Highest honor.*

"What are you doing?" Maisie asked Curly's father.

Worm did not stop piling sod when he answered, "Building a sweat lodge."

"Like a sauna?" Maisie asked.

Worm looked at her and shrugged. "For purification," he said.

"Purification of what?"

Worm sighed. "You ask too many questions," he said gently. He wiped his hands on his shirt.

"Very important for boys to go on vision quest," he explained, lowering himself to the ground.

He tapped the spot beside him for Maisie to sit. When she did, he continued.

"He purifies in sweat lodge, then goes off alone

for four days with no food or water. Hopefully, a vision will come to him. The shaman interprets this vision, which will give the boy direction. It will show him what he must do in his life."

Maisie grabbed Worm's hand. "I want to go on a vision quest," she said urgently.

He smiled. "Only boys."

"But I need direction," Maisie pleaded. "I need help."

"Girls don't go alone," Worm told her. "Someone from the tribe has to go with her. And she must eat and drink. She must work, too. Then the shaman tells her what her spirit guide is before her ceremony."

"Yes," Maisie said. "A spirit guide is exactly what I need."

Worm nodded. "This is done before the girl gets married."

"Married!" Maisie exclaimed. "I'm only twelve years old!"

Worm nodded again. "Women help prepare you with fine new clothes and—"

"You don't understand," Maisie said. "I want to do it like the boys."

Worm patted her hand. Then he stood and went

back to preparing the sweat lodge.

Frustrated, Maisie stomped away. But almost immediately she ran into Curly, who was walking quickly toward his father.

He ignored Maisie—*Of course,* Maisie thought as he hurried past her as if she wasn't standing practically right in his way—and shouted to his father.

"There's no time for that!"

Worm turned toward Curly, puzzled.

"There are white soldiers approaching," Curly said. "We must move on."

But Worm shook his head firmly. "You must have your vision quest."

"It is different now, Father," Curly said sadly.

"First, I will teach you. Then you will go in sweat lodge for purification."

With each thing his father said, Curly's jaw set even harder.

"Then," Worm continued, "you will jump into the river. Then—"

"There's no time!" Curly said, his voice hard and angry.

Felix came up beside Maisie, still beaming with accomplishment.

"I got a first coup," he said, boasting. "Went right up to the scariest Comanche and—"

"Ssshhh," Maisie ordered him.

"You need to find your spirit guide," Worm was saying. "You need to find your way."

"Fine," Curly said. "I will go on my vision quest right now."

"Now?" Worm said, surprised.

"I believe the Great Mystery will understand," Curly said.

"What's going on?" Felix whispered.

But Maisie didn't answer.

"You are not ready now, son."

"Watch me," Curly said.

With that, he turned and began to walk off, away from his father and the village.

Maisie did not hesitate. If Curly could break all the rules and go off on his vision quest, then so could she.

CHAPTER 8

Vision Quest

Curly spun around angrily.

"A vision quest is done alone," he told Maisie. His hands made a shooing motion.

"I won't bother you," she said. "I need to know my life path, too," she added.

"Your life path?" Curly spat. "You and your people will take our land. Kill our buffalo. Kill our people."

"No!" Maisie said, shaking her head even though she knew that of course he was right. White settlers did take land and kill the buffalo. She shivered, remembering the attack at Yellow Feather's village just a day ago.

"Leave me alone," Curly said. He turned away from Maisie and continued to walk away.

Maisie looked around. The craggy white rocks jutted out of the ground, seeming to cut into the sky. It was so quiet here that she shivered again in the silence. She didn't want to go back to the village, and she didn't want to stay here alone. That meant she had to follow Curly, even if he didn't like it.

She kept a good distance behind him as he moved swiftly through the trees. Eventually, Curly came to a stop. Maisie watched him survey the area around him. Satisfied, he sat on the ground, his back straight, his head held high. If this was where Curly believed he would have a vision, then Maisie believed she would get one here, too.

She sat on the warm grass and waited.

After only ten minutes, Maisie heard twigs snapping behind her. Could this be her spirit guide already? she wondered eagerly.

Slowly, she turned to see what her spirit guide was. She imagined a wolf, a snake, an owl.

But instead, she found Felix standing there, sweating and panting.

"Is this the spot?" he asked.

"People go on vision quests alone," Maisie told him, disappointed.

"Really? Then why did you follow Curly?"

"Because I didn't know where to go, that's why," Maisie said. She closed her eyes, pretending her brother hadn't just showed up.

"I'll just sit over there and wait for my vision," Felix said.

Maisie peered out beneath her eyelids as Felix scampered off. She lost sight of him quickly. Good. He didn't need a spirit guide or a vision to find out his life's direction. His path was set: class president, Mr. Popularity, friend to everyone. She was the one who needed guidance, not Felix.

Minutes ticked away.

Then hours.

Maisie's legs grew numb, and she stood to shake out the pins and needles. How would she ever last out here for four days like this?

The sun was getting low in the sky. Soon night would fall. It would be cold. And dark.

Maisie tried to remember if she had ever been completely alone before. The idea frightened her.

Felix is somewhere nearby, she reminded herself.

Maybe it would be okay if she moved just a little bit closer to him, she decided. Careful not to make noise, she walked along until she spotted her brother through the trees. Curly was up that hill, and Felix was right over there in a clearing. Satisfied, she sat back down and waited. Who would have imagined that going on a vision quest was so boring?

She watched as Felix stretched out on the grass and stared up at the sky.

That seemed like a good idea, Maisie thought.

She stretched out, too, and stared up at the pines. It was hard to really see anything. Of course Felix had picked a better spot, a clearing with wide-open spaces. He would be able to see birds and deer and just about anything. And Curly was up on a hill, with a view that went on for miles. She was never going to have a vision here.

Frustrated, Maisie got up and moved closer to Felix. She sat at the edge of the trees but on the grass where the clearing began. Yes, she decided, this was better. Once again she stretched out and stared up at the unobstructed sky. It had turned from blue to every shade of purple as the sun set.

Pretty, Maisie thought.

She waited.

Felix woke with a start. All around him was blackness. Usually he would be afraid alone in the dark like this. But for some reason that he couldn't understand, he felt calm. When he looked up into the sky, it was illuminated with a warm glow from the moon. The stars twinkled above him, and wispy clouds moved past. He had never really seen a face in the moon before, but tonight he could make out kindly eyes, a sharp nose, even a wide mouth.

"Hello, moon," Felix said softly.

He sat up, stretching his back. Sleeping on the ground was not comfortable at all, and he ached everywhere.

Felix thought he heard footsteps. He listened hard. Yes, those were footsteps.

"Maisie?" he said, his voice sounding small in the night.

The footsteps stopped.

"Curly?" he asked into the dark.

The feeling of calm that he'd had moments earlier disappeared. He tried not to think of all the things that might be out here. Wild animals. Angry Comanche. Poisonous snakes.

"Hello?" he squeaked.

The footsteps resumed, pounding toward him.

A tall figure appeared in front of him. Felix could just make out the shape of what looked like a man walking slightly hunched over.

"Curly?" he said again, even though this guy seemed much bigger than Curly.

Felix blinked.

This guy was much, *much* bigger than Curly.

Suddenly, the figure dropped to all fours and moved slowly toward Felix, who scooted backward, feeling rocks and twigs scrape against his bottom.

Now it was only ten feet away, and it once again got to its feet, towering over Felix in the darkness.

Felix looked up and up, straight into the face of a brown bear.

He tried to think of what a person was supposed to do when they saw a bear. Once, he and his father had watched a *National Geographic* television special about bears. He couldn't remember if he should climb a tree or roll into a ball and play dead. But he could remember that there were thirty bear attacks a year on people. *There must have been a lot more back in the 1800s,* Felix thought. Then he realized that the bear wasn't coming any closer.

It just stood there, staring at him.

Felix wondered if it could actually hear his heart, which was pounding so loud that it rang in Felix's ears.

The bear dropped to all fours again.

And then it turned around and walked away.

Felix stared after it in disbelief.

He sat, trying to slow his breathing, waiting for the fear to leave his body. When he finally stopped trembling, a thought came to him.

"Maisie!" Felix called, scrambling to his feet. "I just had my vision!"

Maisie was asleep when she heard Felix calling her name. She jolted awake. Something must have happened to him. His voice was so shrill and excited she couldn't make out what he was saying.

Wait. Did he just say something about a bear?

She started to run in his direction, until she almost bumped right into him.

"It's a bear!" Felix was shouting.

When she heard what he said next, Maisie's heart fell.

"My spirit guide is a bear!"

"You saw something?" Maisie asked.

Felix nodded. "A giant brown bear. Maybe ten feet tall on two legs. He came right up to me and just stood there staring."

"You probably dreamed that," Maisie said.

"No, no," he insisted. "It was *huge*. And it was *real*."

"Well, good for you," Maisie said, and she stomped off as noisily as she could, back to her spot.

"Wait!" Felix said, hurrying to catch up to her. "What do you think it means?"

"That you're over*bear*ing, maybe," she said. "Leave me alone. I need to have my own vision."

"Maisie," Felix said, and she caught a glimpse of him standing helplessly, his hands raised as if in surrender, before she lost sight of him in the dark.

Maisie's stomach grumbled with hunger. She could see red berries hanging from nearby bushes, and nuts littered the ground. But she refused to eat anything. The idea was to go without food or water for four days. If that was what it took for a real vision quest, then Maisie was going to do it, even though she felt dizzy and weak after just two nights. So dizzy and weak that she tripped easily over a rock and landed hard on her back.

Tears sprang to her eyes.

After Felix woke her up, she'd spent the rest of that night angry at the unfairness of life. She hadn't fallen back asleep until the sun came up. Then she'd wandered, dispirited and hungry, studying the rocks and the trees, desperate for a sign, an omen, anything.

Last night she'd fallen asleep soon after dark, and she had woken this morning disappointed. No bear had come to her. Nothing had. She hadn't even had a dream. And now here she was, flat on her back, defeated. Hot tears stung her eyes and rolled down her cheeks.

You'll get tears in your ears from crying on your back.

Maisie balked. She thought she heard her father's voice, as clear as if he were standing somewhere nearby.

She listened hard. But all she heard was the wind whistling across the plains.

Sighing, she stared up at the blue, cloudless sky and watched as a bird made lazy loops above her. It almost seemed that with every loop, the bird came closer to the earth. No, it *was* coming closer, she realized. She could see its sleek, gray body clearly now. With a few more circles, she could make out its long, pointed feathers. And then she could even see its small face and beak.

A hawk, Maisie thought.

As soon as she thought that, she felt her pulse quicken. Was this it? Her spirit guide?

The bird slowed.

Maisie could actually hear its wings slicing through the air.

Suddenly, the bird was close enough for her to touch it.

Maisie held her breath.

The bird glided just above her, its wings brushing her face.

It seemed to hover there for a long minute before it reversed, making its lazy loops upward and away until it became just a speck far up in the sky.

Maisie lay there, straining to see it in the sunlight. Long after she could not find it there any longer, she stayed motionless, the touch of the bird's wings still on her cheeks.

Maisie's elation over her vision quickly evaporated

when she finally returned to the village and found the women taking down the tepees.

"What's happening?" she asked Felix as soon as she saw him.

"They're moving," he said. "They heard that the soldiers are coming."

Maisie and Felix watched as the women removed the buffalo hides and dismantled the poles.

"There's Curly," Felix said, pointing. "He's been with his father."

Curly saw them, too, and walked over to Maisie and Felix, his eyes glazed and distant.

"Once my father got over being angry at me for not doing the proper rituals, he interpreted my vision," Curly said, slightly dazed.

"What was your vision?" Felix asked him.

Curly shook his head, as if he was trying to clear it. Then he spoke slowly.

"I saw a horseman floating above me. He had long, light hair that blew in the wind. Hair like mine. The horse was dancing, and the man was not painted at all. I have never seen a warrior like this. He was plain, and he told me that I, too, should not adorn myself. Just a small brown stone behind my ear."

At this, Curly lightly touched a spot behind his ear before he continued.

"I saw a battle. The horseman's arms were held by his own people, yet neither arrows nor bullets touched him."

Again, Curly shook his head, trying to make sense of this vision.

"He said that I must take a handful of dust from our sacred ground and sprinkle it on my horse before battle, and then I must rub it into my skin and hair."

Curly rubbed his arm.

"And he told me that after battle, I must never keep anything for myself. I must never boast about my victories."

"Wow," Felix said. "All I saw was a big bear."

Curly smiled. "A bear is a good spirit guide, Felix. It tells you to be more tolerant and to keep your optimism. It tells you to stop finding fault with people and things around you."

"What does your vision mean?" Maisie asked. "What did your father say?"

"He listened carefully," Curly said, his voice serious. "He said to listen to my vision. To dress plainly. To put the stone behind my ear. To throw dust on my horse before battle and on myself as well. He said I should be a man of charity. He said that I could only be injured if one of my own people holds my arms. And he said that people would sing about my courage someday. That I would be a brave warrior."

Maisie and Felix stood awed by the importance of Curly's vision and his father's interpretation.

"Did you have a vision?" Curly asked Maisie.

"A gray hawk with pointed wings came to me," Maisie said, touching the place on her cheek where she'd felt its wings.

Curly laughed. "Hawks are red with rounded wings. You saw a falcon."

"What does a falcon mean?" Maisie asked him.

"Your life path is individuality," Curly said. "You must learn patience with those who don't understand that."

"Really?" Maisie said, as a feeling of peace came over her.

Felix was thinking hard. Listening to Curly describe his vision and his father's interpretation of it, something had struck him hard. Curly was told not to be boastful about his accomplishments, to let others sing about his victories. This lesson seemed like one that Felix needed to learn, too. Hadn't he betrayed Maisie because he thought he was better than her in some ways?

Emotion tore through him, and he grabbed his sister hard and held her in a tight hug.

Curly looked at them knowingly.

"The vision quest teaches us many things," he said.

He turned to leave, but then returned as if he had forgotten something.

"The horseman," Curly said, "he instructed me to wear a single red-tailed hawk feather instead of a warbonnet. A warrior without a warbonnet," he added.

Maisie and Felix looked at each other.

"I think it's time," Felix said softly.

But Maisie was now searching the empty space where the tepees had been. Yellow Feather and the women had finished taking them down, and there was nothing left where she and Felix had slept.

"Maisie," Felix said. "The feather."

Maisie looked back at Felix, then at Curly, before

she broke into a run. Somehow she had to find whoever took down that tepee and the small bag that had been hanging on the post. The bag where she'd hidden the red-tailed hawk feather.

CHAPTER 9

Brave Warrior

Maisie stared in the empty space where the tepee had stood. How would she ever track down that bag? Without it, there was no way back home. Strange, Maisie thought, just a few days ago Newport, Rhode Island, was the last place she wanted to be. But something about her vision quest and the falcon made her feel more comfortable in her own skin. Her life path, Curly had said, was individuality. Perhaps if she stopped caring about Bitsy Beal and Avery Mason and the rest of them, she might be able to follow her life path, whatever that meant.

But if she didn't find that bag, she wouldn't get the opportunity to find out.

She didn't realize that Curly had followed her.

He was standing beside her now, looking confused and displeased.

"There was a bag," Maisie began. "Hanging on one of the poles in the tepee."

Curly looked even more displeased.

"The medicine bundle?" he demanded.

"I . . . I don't think so," Maisie said. "It didn't have medicine in it."

"You looked inside?" Curly said angrily.

"I wanted a safe place to put something," Maisie tried explaining. But Curly was not listening.

He folded his arms across his chest and glared at her.

"That was my father's medicine bundle," he said. "No one except the medicine man and my father knows what is inside it. Now its power is destroyed. Useless."

"I'm sorry," Maisie said.

Curly glared at her.

"The only reason you were allowed to stay is because the Lakota share their food, their tepees. My father insisted, even though I told him I do not trust the white settlers. Even young ones like you."

"I'm so sorry," Maisie said again, close to tears.

"Where is the medicine bundle?"

"My father has it with him. He will need it as we move past the settlers."

"Maybe I can talk to the medicine man and make it powerful again?" Maisie said hopefully.

"Ha!" Curly snorted. "Do you have two or three horses for a new medicine bundle?"

"No."

"Then you cannot help," he said dismissively. "You've done enough damage. It is time for you to go off on your own. Back to your people."

With that he turned on his heel, away from her.

"I can't go back without what I put in that bag!" Maisie shouted after him.

Curly stopped. He turned around slowly, his eyes steely.

"What did you put in there?" he asked evenly.

"A . . . a feather," Maisie said.

By now, Felix had joined them.

"You lost the feather?" he said.

Maisie nodded.

"What is so important about this feather?" Curly asked Felix.

"It's from home," Felix said carefully. "It's hard to

explain, but we need to give it to you in order to go back."

Curly's face grew thoughtful.

"This feather has power?" he asked finally.

"Yes," Felix and Maisie both answered.

He seemed to consider this carefully.

"Come," he said to them. "We will go to my father and seek his advice."

"How could you do something like that?" Felix whispered to Maisie as they walked across the empty field.

By now, the people were loading their horses with their belongings, preparing to leave.

They found Worm throwing buffalo hides onto a horse and securing them with rawhide.

"Father," Curly said. "Do you have your medicine bundle?"

Worm shook his head no.

"What?" Maisie exclaimed. "Where is it?"

"Little Thunder borrowed it," Worm said, surprised by Maisie's reaction. "He needed good luck."

"But where is Little Thunder?" Felix asked.

Worm shrugged and pointed toward the horizon.

"Gone," he said simply.

Frightened, Maisie looked at Felix. He looked back at her, fear in his eyes.

Curly said, "Little Thunder does need good luck. Your feather will give him special power."

"No, no," Felix said. "You don't understand. *We* need that feather."

"To give to me," Curly said.

"Right," Felix said.

"I give it to him," Curly said, satisfied.

"You can't," Maisie insisted.

Worm spoke softly, his voice tinged with sadness.

"Four summers ago, a great council met at Fort Laramie to end the government's intrusion on our land and our people. They insisted we choose a chief, someone to tell us what to do. All of us! The Lakota and the Crow and the Cheyenne, the Arapaho and Shoshone. As if one man could order so many different people."

Worm paused, considering this idea before he continued.

"Since we do not believe in such a person, the government chose for us. They gave us presents and money so that the white settlers could move safely along the Holy Road. They were satisfied with this. But no one, not Conquering Bear, who they named chief, not me, no one, rules the Lakota."

He set his dark eyes directly on Maisie.

"No one rules the Lakota because we own nothing and nobody. You see?"

"I understand," Maisie said, "but—"

"Little Thunder needed good luck," Worm reminded her.

She watched as he climbed on his horse and slowly joined the tribe as they left what had been their village.

"How can we find Little Thunder?" Felix asked Curly.

"You can ride with us," Curly said, his voice heavy with resignation. "Maybe we see him. Maybe not."

"Arapaho," a voice whispered to Curly through the tepee flaps a few nights later.

They had ridden for days across the plains before finally setting up their tepees. Maisie and Felix were so dispirited that they did not even feel relieved to be off horseback and on the soft buffalo hides, gazing up at the stars through the opening at the very top of the tepee. Without that feather, they were trapped here in 1800s, out in the Great Plains, with no hope of getting back home to Newport.

Curly sat up.

"Are they planning a raid?" Curly asked.

"In the morning," came the answer.

Then the sound of footsteps hurrying away.

Maisie shivered despite the warm blanket covering her. She thought of her bed in the Princess Room, with its supersoft sheets and silk canopy. She thought about the big pink poufe, and how she liked to sink into it and think her thoughts. All of those things seemed impossibly far away, and Maisie feared she would never see Elm Medona, or her mother, again.

"We must prepare for battle," Curly said to Felix.

"Battle?" Felix sputtered.

"Maybe get good horses," Curly added.

Felix thought about the day they had gone to touch the enemy. He still could clearly see the face of the Comanche, his bow drawn, the arrow aimed at Felix. In a battle, that arrow would be fired.

"Curly, I don't want to fight," Felix said, trying to

hide the trembling in his voice.

Curly stood before them both, dressed simply. On his cheek he'd painted a white zigzag that looked like a lightning bolt, but nothing more.

"We attack Arapaho before they attack us," he said matter-of-factly.

He waited until Felix reluctantly got up. Curly reached forward and painted white spots on Felix's face.

"Hail," he said when he'd finished. "Like the hail of our arrows on the Arapaho."

In the moonlight streaming in from the top of the tepee, Curly's and Felix's faces glowed eerily.

Maisie jumped up.

"I can't let him go alone," she said.

"Girls do not come on raids," Curly told her.

"Stay, Maisie," Felix said. "It's too dangerous."

"If you're going, I'm going," Maisie insisted.

"In a dress?" Curly said, pointing at her.

"Get me leggings. And a shirt," Maisie said firmly.

Curly hesitated, then left the tepee.

"You don't have any idea how scary it is," Felix said.

"I saw the attack on Yellow Feather's village," she reminded him. "I'll never forget it."

Curly returned and handed her buckskin leggings and a shirt with a white sun painted on the front.

"Power," he said, showing her the circle there.

"I'll be right out," Maisie said.

The clothes smelled like the suede jacket her father used to wear. He'd bought it long ago at a flea market in Rome, and it had been one of his prized possessions. Maisie used to like to bury her head in his chest and smell the rich scent mixed with a long-ago owner's tobacco. She wondered if he'd taken that jacket with him to Qatar, where it was always hot and no one ever needed to wear jackets. Like so many things from their old lives in New York, it had probably been discarded. Maisie was probably the only one of the four of them who even thought about it so fondly. Everyone else just kept moving on, as if their lives together on Bethune Street didn't matter anymore.

Sighing, she stepped out of her dress and into the leggings and shirt. The clothes felt heavy, the rich smell enveloping her. Maisie reached into the pocket of her dress and pulled out the elastic she always carried but never used on her unruly hair. But now she gathered it into a thick ponytail and tucked the ends under the elastic, hoping she looked a little bit more like a boy.

Then she stepped out of the tepee, where, as far as she could see, bare-chested warriors sat erect on horseback.

Her eyes scanned the group until she found Felix and Curly. Beside them, a white-and-black-spotted horse waited for her. Curly watched her struggle onto it. But she did it, finally settling into the curve of its back. In the distance, the sun was beginning to rise, the blazing orange ball on the horizon.

Curly raised his hand and let out a war cry, high-pitched and ferocious.

The others responded with whooping and cries.

With a thunder of hooves and a cloud of dust swirling around them, Maisie and Felix were off to battle.

The Lakota warriors charged forward, directly into the Arapaho preparing to attack. The Arapaho wore large feathered warbonnets, like the Lakota. But the Arapaho warriors wore elaborate fringed shirts decorated with colorful beads, lines of porcupine quills, and rows of elk's teeth. Their faces were painted with bright war paint. Except for Curly, who painted just the lightning bolt on his cheek, the Lakota also painted their faces and bodies with bright colors and sacred designs. They painted their horses, too, and attached feathers to their tails. The bravest warriors wore fur necklaces and sashes across their bare chests. Maisie noticed they all had their medicine bundles tied to their breeches or to the horses' tails, and she thought longingly of the feather she'd tucked into Worm's medicine bundle.

Hump, one of the fiercest Lakota warriors, led the charge, with Curly close behind him. A barrage of arrows were shot at them as they approached the enemy. Suddenly, Hump's horse was shot from under him. Arapaho warriors quickly converged on him as he fell to the ground. Maisie thought for sure they were going to kill Hump, but as the arrows continued to fly, Curly leaped off his own horse and in one quick motion lifted Hump from the ground and away from the arrows of the Arapaho.

"How did he do that?" Felix said in wonder as Curly managed to get Hump on his own horse with him and continue to keep moving, the Arapaho keeping stride.

Curly fearlessly rode straight through the enemy lines even as arrows whizzed past him.

Maisie and Felix hung back, watching the battle rage ahead of them. It seemed like the arrows could not hurt Curly, even though he was in the middle of the fighting. The warriors noticed it, too, and soon the Arapaho were retreating. The Lakota began a war chant, circling Curly and rhythmically bowing to him from atop their horses in admiration and respect.

Suddenly, out of nowhere, two Arapaho warriors thundered up to him, challenging Curly face-to-face, their bows and arrows poised to kill.

Maisie held her breath. The moment felt like hours.

An arrow let loose, heading directly for Curly's heart.

But it missed by a hair, brushing past him and landing in the grass.

Just as Maisie exhaled, Curly shot off two arrows in rapid succession. The first killed the warrior who had shot at him. The second took down the other challenger. Both men looked surprised when they were hit. Each of them grabbed at the arrow in his chest, as if he couldn't believe it was there. And then, in slow motion, their eyes rolled back in their heads, and first one, then the other, slumped forward on his horse.

Curly urged his own horse close to them.

In horror, Maisie and Felix watched as he lifted up the first warrior's head by the hair with one hand, and raised his tomahawk high in the other, slicing the air as the tomahawk cleanly scalped the fallen Arapaho.

Felix had to look away, but Maisie could not stop watching as Curly did the same to the second dead warrior.

He lifted the bloody scalps for everyone to see.

Then he began to attach them to his belt.

Just then, an arrow flew through the air and hit Curly straight in the leg.

His body jerked with surprise and a look of pain filled his face.

Without hesitating, Hump yanked the arrow from Curly's leg.

"Ouch!" Maisie blurted.

Even from where they sat on their horses, she could see the blood spurting.

Hump bent and placed a piece of rawhide on the wound.

The warriors were chanting and whooping even louder now.

"He got hit because he was keeping the scalps," Felix said. "Remember his vision?"

Maisie nodded. "He isn't supposed to keep anything for himself."

They watched as Curly threw the scalps to the ground. Then he turned on his horse and gave a loud, victorious cry. Even the most decorated warriors surrounded him and bowed.

The Arapaho had retreated, and Curly had become a hero.

CHAPTER 10

Crazy Horse

Excitement rippled through the village upon their return. News about the battle had already spread, and by the time they rode back to camp, everyone knew that Curly had saved Hump, one of the most honored and most ferocious warriors in their tribe. Arrows, they'd been told, seemed to bounce off Curly. He had killed two Arapaho up close, scalping them easily.

As the warriors entered the camp, the entire tribe greeted them.

Standing in the front was Worm, waiting for his son.

Curly dismounted and approached his father, who placed a hand on each of Curly's shoulders. He looked him in the eye.

"For someone so young," he said solemnly, "you have shown remarkable bravery."

Curly stood proudly before his people, but said nothing.

"You have a wound," Worm said, indicating where the arrow had struck his leg.

"I did not listen to my dream," Curly admitted. "In the heat of victory, I took scalps and kept them for myself."

Worm nodded. "You will not forget that lesson again."

"No, Father," Curly said. "I won't."

Worm faced the tribe and announced, "Tonight I will have a ceremony for my son, to honor his bravery today, and to send him forward with a new name worthy of his warrior status."

A murmur spread through the crowd. Almost immediately, they dispersed to make preparations for the ceremony. Women began to light a fire in the center of the camp. They retrieved buffalo meat, baskets of fruits and vegetables. Others prepared special ceremonial robes and bonnets.

Maisie and Felix watched all of the activity swirling around them.

"He really was brave," Felix said.

"Yes," Maisie agreed, feeling miserable.

"I know," Felix said. "It's time to leave."

"But we might never get out of here!" Maisie blurted.

"We won't be stuck, Maisie," Felix said. "Don't worry. There has to be a way to find Little Thunder."

But he didn't really believe that. As far as he could tell, there was no way to find Little Thunder and no way to get back home.

They sat together watching everyone preparing for the ceremony, wishing more than anything that somehow they could close their eyes and find themselves tumbling through time again.

"Maisie," Felix said later that afternoon, "maybe we can figure out another way back."

They had watched everyone busily preparing for the ceremony for a long time. But without anything to do themselves, they'd decided to take a walk down by the river. Standing there now, even the sight of rainbow trout jumping through the air and splashing back into the water, and the way the sunlight made the river sparkle, could not lift their gloom.

Maisie didn't even look at Felix. The idea was ridiculous, she knew. They had to give the feather to Curly in order to go home. And the feather was gone.

"I've been thinking," Felix continued, "and maybe the object isn't the thing that gets us back."

"Then why did Great-Aunt Maisie keep those handcuffs for so long?"

Had he forgotten how Great-Aunt Maisie schemed to time travel to meet Harry Houdini again? How she'd kept those handcuffs just so she could do that?

"She kept them to *go back*," Felix said.

"Right," Maisie said, frustrated. "What's your point?"

"The objects bring us back in time," Felix said patiently. "They don't bring us home. They stay with the person. Clara kept the letter, and Alexander kept the coin, and Pearl—"

"You're right!" Maisie said, finally understanding. "But if the feather brought us here, then what will bring us home?"

"That's what I've been thinking about," Felix said. "And I may have figured it out."

Now Maisie was studying her brother's face closely, waiting to hear what he had to say.

"Everything we tried to go home failed, right?" he asked.

But he didn't wait for an answer.

"I thought real hard today about what happened right before we traveled back. With Clara, she was telling us about *her* great-aunt, and how we should pay more attention to Great-Aunt Maisie."

"Okay," Maisie said as she tried to remember. "And Alexander and I were in that cemetery—"

"And he told you how important family was. He was an orphan, and he knew how hard—"

"Pearl talked about losing her sisters and brothers—"

"And Harry told me: *I believe in you. Now you just have to believe in yourself,*" Maisie said, growing excited.

"The thing is," Felix said, "he said it to you, but it meant something to me, too. I wanted to win the election for class president and to have friends, and even though it was all going so well, I didn't believe in myself yet. He gave me the courage to really put myself out there."

"We just wanted different things," Maisie said softly. She still couldn't accept that after being together their whole lives and moving along the same path, she and Felix now wanted different things.

"We're twins," Felix said, "but we're individuals, too."

Maisie nodded sadly.

"We'll always be twins," he added, throwing his arm around her shoulders. And as much as he had wanted to un-twin, the fact that he was always going to be Maisie's twin brother suddenly felt perfect.

"I guess that's what our vision quest was all about," he said.

"Tolerance *and* individuality," Maisie agreed.

Felix looked at Maisie, his eyes wide.

"But that means we did get a lesson from Curly. He interpreted our spirit guides for us."

Maisie felt her hopes crashing. "And we're still here," she said.

"What are we missing?" Felix asked.

But Maisie didn't answer. She knew it was another rhetorical question.

The sound of a stone dropping into the water caught their attention.

Down the bank a bit, Yellow Feather stood skipping stones. Maisie and Felix watched as she lightly threw a stone across the water, and it skimmed the surface, alighting once, twice, three times before landing with a pleasant plop.

"Can you show me how to do that?" Felix called to her.

Yellow Feather's face brightened when she saw them.

"It's simple," she said. "Come."

"Learning how to skip stones isn't going to help us figure out how to get home," Maisie said.

"Neither is standing here," Felix reminded her.

Yellow Feather handed Felix a smooth, round stone, and demonstrated how to throw it in such a way that it didn't land immediately but rather danced across the water.

"You try," Felix told Maisie when he finally got a stone to skim across the surface. "It's kind of like throwing a Frisbee."

Maisie took the stone he offered her and pretended she was in Central Park playing Frisbee with her father. He had taken Maisie and Felix there on summer afternoons, patiently teaching them the fine art of throwing a Frisbee.

But when she tried it with the stone, it just landed with a splash.

"Practice," Yellow Feather said. "You can do it."

But every stone Maisie threw just belly flopped into the river, while Felix's gracefully skimmed along.

"I give up," Maisie said finally.

She took one last rock and imagined her father standing across the green grass in Central Park, smiling at her. *You can do it, Maisie!* he'd say, and that Frisbee would leave her hand and float right into his.

"Look!" Felix shouted.

Maisie did look, and her stone touched down on the water, then lifted ever so slightly, before gently dropping into the river.

"I'm glad you found me here," Yellow Feather said. "I am sad, and you made me happy."

"Why are you sad?" Felix asked her.

"I want to find my people. I want to go home."

"So do we!" Maisie said.

"Little Thunder was supposed to take me," Yellow Feather said. "But he is gone."

"Do you think he'll come back for you?" Felix asked hopefully.

But Yellow Feather shook her head no.

The sun was sinking low on the horizon now. Without it shining down on them, the air grew cold quickly, and the shadows grew long.

"We need to return for the ceremony," Yellow Feather said.

The three of them slowly walked away from the river, up the hill toward the village. Each of them homesick. Each of them deep in private thought, trying to figure out a way home.

The tribe was dressed in full celebration regalia. All of the clothing was painted in bright colors with circles representing the sun, eagles, wolves, and other symbols of strength and power. The men wore headdresses thick with feathers that trailed down their backs. A fire blazed in the center of the village, and behind it drummers banged out a rhythmic beat. The air was thick with smoke and the smells of buffalo meat roasting and sage burning.

In the crowd, Maisie and Felix could see Curly. He was unadorned, his hair loose and his face decorated with only the lightning bolt on his cheek.

Around him, the tribe began to gather in a circle.

Yellow Feather urged Maisie and Felix to come with her as she joined the circle. Their bodies pressed tight together as they fell into step with the chanting, dancing people.

Felix easily followed their movements. As his body bent, dipped, then straightened again, he remembered dancing with Lily Goldberg at Bitsy Beal's party. That night seemed so long ago now, but Felix could still feel Lily's hand in his, and the joy he'd felt standing beside her doing the chicken dance and the twist. Maisie, too, picked up the simple movements of the dancing circle, but she felt more awkward as she followed their steps. Would she ever be comfortable in her skin the way Felix seemed to be? She tried to focus on Curly's interpretation of her vision of the falcon. Didn't that promise her a happy, independent future?

The dancing went on and on, everyone's bodies growing sweaty as they moved around the roaring fire. The chanting intensified, and time began to blur in a swirl of sound and motion and aromas.

Hypnotized, Felix felt like he might faint. His ears rang and he was light-headed. In this state, he thought of that red-tailed hawk feather. It seemed to float in front of him, and he lifted his hand as if he could grab it from the air. But his hand fell through the emptiness and landed on Maisie's sweaty back.

The feather.

Felix gasped.

He understood now. The feather had brought them here. And Curly had given them what they needed to go home. But their original idea had been right: The missing step was to give Curly the feather. All Felix had figured out was the basic steps. They needed the shard from the Ming vase at Elm Medona. An object from The Treasure Chest allowed them to time travel. They needed to give the object to the right person. That person had to give them something in return.

His mind swirled with images of Clara and Alexander and Pearl and Harry.

And Curly.

"We need to give Curly the feather," Felix said out loud, but his words were lost in the sounds of the ceremony.

When Worm separated from the group and began to speak, it took a moment for everyone to stop and listen.

But it came just in time for Felix, who wondered if he could make himself move even one more inch. He staggered, and then half fell to the ground.

Maisie kneeled beside him.

He was too weak to explain everything to her.

"My son," Worm intoned. "Brave warrior."

At the sound of those words, the tribe let loose a series of cries and hollers.

Curly stood beside his father, his head bent humbly.

"As a boy," Worm continued, "we called him Curly."

A murmur of acknowledgment rippled through the crowd.

"His hair is unusual," Worm said.

Everyone nodded in unison.

"It does not fly straight, like ours," Worm said. "It is not dark like the night."

Again, the crowd agreed.

"He loves our people," Worm said.

The sounds of appreciation grew louder.

"He loves our homeland," Worm said, his voice louder so that he could be heard over the deafening sounds of the tribe.

"Today, he killed two Arapaho face-to-face! Today he rescued Hump, one of our bravest warriors! Today he showed his bravery without hesitation!"

Felix's face burned from the heat of the fire and the excitement around him. He felt too weak to stand again, but he managed to lift his head to watch the rest of the ceremony.

"Tonight, we honor him!" Worm said.

Maisie's eyes were wide at the sight in front of her. The Lakota singing Curly's praises, Curly standing bare chested and bare headed before them.

"Tonight," Worm shouted above the roar, "I name him Crazy Horse, brave Lakota warrior!"

CHAPTER 11

Losing The Treasure Chest

The naming ceremony went long into the night. Well after midnight, Maisie and Felix found themselves in the tepee, snuggled beneath blankets of buffalo skins. The moon shone through the opening at the top of the tepee, illuminating it like their nightlights did at home.

Sometime, hours later, Felix awoke to the sounds of a commotion somewhere nearby. His first instinct was to stay put. Already he'd witnessed the attack on Yellow Feather's village and the battle with the Arapaho. The images of that destruction and warfare were enough to keep him away from any signs of trouble. But as he lay there listening to the noise outside, Felix became certain that whatever was happening was a happy thing.

He nudged Maisie awake. She grumbled and muttered, then rolled away from him.

"Wake up," Felix said, shaking her shoulder. "There's a lot of excitement outside."

She was quiet a moment, listening.

"They're *still* celebrating Curly's new name," she said finally.

"No, it's something else," Felix insisted.

"Okay," she said, throwing the blanket off her. She shivered in the chilly night air. "I can't imagine what's happening," she added.

It seemed like a million years ago that Maisie had stomped and thudded around Elm Medona, wanting to be noticed. Ever since they'd arrived on the Great Plains, she wasn't so sure that being heard was always the best idea. The animosity everyone felt toward the white settlers, the danger of battles and attacks, the herds of buffalo everywhere made Maisie want to go *un*noticed.

The fire still roared in the center of the village. It didn't look as if any of the tribe had gone to bed. People were eating and dancing and singing without any sign of stopping.

"See?" Maisie said, ready to turn around and go back to bed.

Felix pointed to a spot away from the gathering, near where the horses were kept. A small, noisy group stood there.

"That's what I heard," he said. Felix squinted in the dark. "I think that's Curly and Yellow Feather."

Felix headed off toward them with Maisie right behind him.

It wasn't until they reached Curly and the others that Felix saw what all the excitement was about.

"Maisie," he said, grabbing his sister's hand. "Look."

Maisie blinked hard, to be sure she was really seeing what she thought she was seeing. She was, she realized with more relief than she'd ever felt in her entire life.

Then Felix said out loud the words ringing in her heart.

"Little Thunder."

Little Thunder brought news of the white settlers. His descriptions of the soldiers attacking villages and killing buffalo, of them going back on the promises they'd made at Fort Laramie, and of their growing numbers caused great excitement. At first, Maisie and Felix just listened to him talk, a terrible feeling of dread spreading through them.

But when Crazy Horse noticed them standing there, his face grew angry.

"You two," he said. "What do you say about Little Thunder's report?"

All eyes turned to Maisie and Felix.

"Um," Felix said. "We . . . we don't have anything to do with any of that."

Crazy Horse stepped closer to Felix, glaring.

"You are a white settler. You kill my people," he said.

The others' voices rose behind him.

"No!" Felix said.

Maisie looked at Little Thunder. He wore the buckskin leggings and shirt that she'd grown accustomed to. And hanging from his belt, beside what appeared to be a scalp, was a medicine bundle.

"Curly," Maisie began.

The voices grew even angrier.

"Have you no respect?" Hump said, his voice cutting through the others. "Tonight, he became Crazy Horse."

"I'm sorry," Maisie said quickly. "I'm not used to people changing their names. I mean Crazy Horse." She swallowed hard.

"Crazy Horse," she began again. "We want to leave as soon as possible. We want . . ." She swallowed again. "We want to go home."

Crazy Horse folded his arms across his chest and waited.

"But we can't do that unless Little Thunder gives us his medicine bundle," Maisie explained.

Everyone began to shout, outraged.

Felix's legs trembled. He wouldn't be surprised if at any minute they attacked him and Maisie. The group surged forward, their faces twisted with rage.

But Crazy Horse lifted his hand to silence them.

"No one can see what is in a warrior's medicine bundle. Only medicine man. And warrior," he said evenly.

"I know, I know," Maisie said quickly, hoping she sounded respectful as well as desperate. "But I did a terrible thing. I had that feather for you and I wanted to keep it safe so I put it in the medicine bundle in the tepee and then your father gave that to Little Thunder and now he's back and I want to give you the feather so that Felix and I can go home."

Her words spilled out like a waterfall, and Maisie watched Crazy Horse struggling to catch them all.

Before he answered, Yellow Feather spoke.

"I, too, want to go back to my village," she said. "I understand."

Crazy Horse turned to Yellow Feather. "It will take Little Thunder's strength if she opens the medicine bundle."

"But she already has," Yellow Feather said. "She opened it and put something inside and still Little Thunder has his power."

Crazy Horse considered this.

"Find my father," he said finally. "He will decide what to do."

He pointed a finger at Felix and Maisie.

"Until he arrives, you stay here."

Felix glanced around. The Lakota had formed a circle around him and his sister. He didn't have a choice. There was no way out.

Worm appeared, looking solemn.

Maisie once again tried to explain.

"You've got to let me open that medicine bundle you gave Little Thunder. Please, please. I didn't know it was a special bag, and I just wanted to keep my present safe," she said, her words coming out in a rush of pleading and desperation. "I didn't know the whole village would move. I didn't know—"

"Little Thunder," Worm said, "give me the medicine bundle."

Little Thunder untied the rawhide bag from his belt and handed it to Worm.

"Come with me," Worm said softly to Maisie.

"Come with you?" Maisie repeated, not sure that she wanted to.

But Worm didn't wait for her to reply. He just walked away, past the group that had gathered, past the horses, and down the grassy slope toward the river.

When he saw that Felix was also following him, he paused.

"You," he said to Felix, "go back."

"But—"

Worm had already turned around and continued on his way to the river.

"Maisie," Felix whispered, "I don't want you to go alone."

"I have to," she said. "It's our only chance."

The truth was that she felt brave and special

going with Worm alone. He was a medicine man, not a warrior. Maisie was certain he wouldn't hurt her. Still, Felix quietly followed many paces behind them. He'd deserted his sister too many times to let her go off alone now.

At the bank of the river, Worm stopped.

He spoke in his native language, his eyes closed, his face tilted toward the moon.

"I have thanked Wakan Tanka, the Great Mystery, for Crazy Horse's bravery," he said when he finished.

He closed his eyes once more and spoke again in his language.

"I have thanked the sun, Wi, for his power," he explained. "And the moon, Winan. It is all *wakan*, mystery, no?" Worm asked her gently.

Maisie nodded. *Wakan*, she thought. *Mystery*.

Worm untied the strings and opened the medicine bundle. When he looked inside, bewilderment crossed his face.

"You brought this for my son?" he asked as he pulled the red-tailed hawk feather from the bag.

"Yes," Maisie said, her eyes filling with tears of relief.

"But how could you know what his vision would tell?"

Maisie didn't know how to answer.

"In his dream," Worm said slowly, "he was told to not wear a warbonnet. He was told to wear a single feather."

Worm waited, but still Maisie could not answer.

"Child," Worm said gently, "where have you come from?"

He tilted her chin upward with his large, square hand so that he could look her in the eye.

"The future," Maisie told him.

Worm studied her with deep concentration. It felt to Maisie that he was actually peering into her brain or even deeper.

Finally, he asked, "Will my people be all right?"

Maisie chewed her bottom lip.

"No," she said at last.

Worm nodded.

"I'm so sorry," Maisie said.

Worm nodded again.

"Bring this to my son," he said. "Give it to Crazy Horse."

Maisie took the feather and began to run up the

grassy hill. When she reached the place where Felix waited, she did not slow down. Felix ran alongside her in the moonlight.

Everyone was standing just as they had left them.

Maisie ran right up to Crazy Horse. She held the feather out to him.

"I'm sorry," she said.

But she would never know if he heard her.

The last thing she and Felix saw was Crazy Horse tucking the red-tailed hawk feather into his long hair.

Then they began to tumble through time.

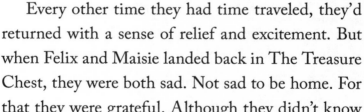

Every other time they had time traveled, they'd returned with a sense of relief and excitement. But when Felix and Maisie landed back in The Treasure Chest, they were both sad. Not sad to be home. For that they were grateful. Although they didn't know what Crazy Horse would go on to do in his lifetime, they both knew the fate of the Lakota, and all of the Native Americans, and knowing that filled them with deep sadness.

Together, they left The Treasure Chest, their hearts heavy.

They climbed down the secret staircase and through the door hidden in the wall.

And walked smack into Great-Uncle Thorne.

He was wearing a tuxedo with a deep purple cummerbund and matching bow tie. His bushy white eyebrows were knitted into an enormous frown.

"Aha!" he roared. "You rapscallions! I knew you'd be up there."

"So what?" Maisie said.

"So what?" Great-Uncle Thorne said. "You've just taken your last trip to The Treasure Chest."

With that, he lifted a heavy lock hanging from an even heavier chain.

"You're locking The Treasure Chest?" Felix asked in disbelief.

"Not only am I locking it," Great-Uncle Thorne said, "tomorrow I have a man coming to seal this door."

Felix and Maisie watched as Great-Uncle Thorne began to ascend the secret staircase.

When he reached the top, he peered down at them from beneath his substantial eyebrows.

"I'm in love!" he announced. *"Amore!"*

"With Penelope Merriweather?" Maisie asked, surprised that someone as handsome and youthful seeming as Great-Uncle Thorne could fall in love with someone as ancient as Penelope Merriweather.

"That's right," Great-Uncle Thorne said, hoisting the lock and chain upward. "And I have to catch up with my beloved's age. The more you two time travel, the longer that will take."

"But—" Felix began.

"Silence!" Great-Uncle Thorne shouted.

Felix and Maisie climbed the secret staircase, too. But before they reached even halfway, Great-Uncle Thorne had attached the lock to the door and fastened it and the chain shut with an ominous click.

"The Treasure Chest," he said gleefully, "is locked permanently."

Crazy Horse

1841–September 5, 1877

No one is certain when Crazy Horse was born, because the Lakota, like most Native Americans, did not keep many written records. However, he was born during a time when the Lakota captured a number of horses from the Shoshone, which likely was in 1841. Historians believe that he was born near Bear Butte, an area in present-day South Dakota, into a Lakota tribe. Little is known about his mother, Rattling Blanket Woman, but his father was a shaman or medicine man. The family did not have any special rank or role in their tribe and lived humbly as ordinary people.

Crazy Horse's light skin and wavy hair led him to be called Light-Skinned Boy and Curly. Even as a young boy he liked to do things his own way. The Lakota were a tolerant people who believed that individuals could follow their own paths. Crazy Horse never participated in ceremonies like the sun ceremony. He also did not participate in the purification rites that most young Lakota men performed. He was a loner, and it is said that he always had a special touch with horses and could break wild horses easily.

When Crazy Horse was born, white settlers had already begun to travel west on the Oregon Trail, which was called the Holy Road by Native Americans. Though there were once millions of buffalo along the trail, by the time Crazy Horse died, almost none were left. He grew up with trepidation of, and then later anger at the white settlers who were taking land, killing buffalo, and attacking villages.

In 1854, a stray cow wandered into a Lakota camp and was killed. That seemingly minor incident is considered a pivotal moment in the tensions between the whites and the Lakota. The cow's owner filed a complaint against the Lakota at Fort Laramie. Lieutenant John Lawrence Grattan, accompanied by thirty-one soldiers, went to the village. Although they were greeted peacefully, the argument escalated, and Grattan ordered that shots be fired. A shot killed Conquering Bear, a Lakota leader. The Lakota retaliated and killed Grattan and all thirty-one soldiers. A year later, six hundred soldiers under General W. S. Harney retaliated by attacking Little Thunder's village, killing eighty-six Native Americans and taking many others captive.

Shortly after the fight with Harney and his men, Crazy Horse went on a vision quest and dreamed of a magical horseman. The horseman told him that he should never adorn himself with war paint. He said that Crazy Horse should wear a single feather instead of a warbonnet, that he should throw dirt on his horse and rub it on himself before battle, and that he should wear a single stone behind his ear. He also said that Crazy Horse should never keep anything for himself. The horseman told him that all Native Americans would sing his praises. Crazy Horse almost always followed these instructions.

After a raid on the Arapaho in which he proved especially brave, his father renamed him Crazy Horse. His reputation as a warrior grew quickly.

The battles that made him famous include what is called Fetterman's Massacre in 1866, which was, at the time, the army's biggest defeat on the Great Plains. In 1876, Crazy Horse led approximately 1,500 warriors in an attack against General George Crook and his 1,000 soldiers. A week later, General George Custer attacked Cheyenne, Arapaho, and Lakota warriors on the Little Bighorn River. That attack marked the beginning of the Battle of the Little Bighorn, which is known as the Battle of the Greasy Grass to the Native Americans. It is also called Custer's Last Stand. The battle was between a combined force of Lakota, Northern Cheyenne, and Arapaho, and the Seventh Cavalry Regiment of the United States Army. The most famous battle of the Great

Sioux War of 1876, it was an overwhelming victory for the Native Americans and a severe defeat for the US Seventh Cavalry, resulting in Custer's death and the loss of hundreds of soldiers. Although Crazy Horse's role in the battle is not clear, everyone agrees that he played a major part. Some historians believe he was the leader of the assault that killed General Custer.

During a brutally cold winter in 1877, Crazy Horse fought his last major battle at Wolf Mountain in Montana Territory. By then, he realized that his time as a free man was coming to an end. His warriors were cold and hungry, and Crazy Horse decided to surrender. He turned himself in to the Red Cloud Agency at Fort Robinson in Nebraska. Until then, he had not understood what a hero he had become. General Crook, worried about Crazy Horse's popularity, ordered him to be arrested. But when they showed up to take him away, Crazy Horse had already fled.

On September 5, 1877, Crazy Horse agreed to return. He believed that during his time at the Red Cloud Agency he had behaved well, and he did not think there were any reasons for him to be arrested. But when he arrived, soldiers were waiting for him and placed him under arrest. Crazy Horse attempted to flee and was fatally stabbed by a bayonet. His body was returned to his father, but his final burial place has never been made public.

Crazy Horse's bravery and dedication to his people and their land made him legendary. In 1948, a sculptor, Korczak Ziolkowski, was commissioned by a Lakota chief named Henry Standing Bear to carve the Crazy Horse Memorial in the Black Hills of South Dakota, near Mount Rushmore where the faces of four US presidents are carved into the mountains. Standing Bear's mission was to honor Crazy Horse and the culture, traditions, and heritage of all Native Americans. The sculpture is still not completed, though work continues on it today.

I do so much research for each book in The Treasure Chest series and discover so many cool facts that I can't fit into every book. Here are some of my favorites from my research for *The Treasure Chest: #5 Crazy Horse: Brave Warrior.* Enjoy!

The world during Crazy Horse's lifetime:

In 1831, about ten years before Crazy Horse was born, President Andrew Jackson began the forced relocation of the Five Civilized Tribes—the Cherokee, Muscogee, Chickasaw, Seminole, and Choctaw—from their southeastern homelands to what is now Oklahoma. En route to their destinations, many Native Americans died from exposure, disease, and starvation. The Choctaw were the first to be relocated. Between 2,500 and 6,000 of 17,000 Choctaws died, leading many to name this event the Trail of Tears.

While Native Americans were being driven off their land, black slaves were fighting for their rights, too.

In 1849, Harriet Tubman escaped from slavery and

joined the Underground Railroad, a secret network of routes and safe houses that helped escaped slaves get to free states.

But just eight years later, the Supreme Court announced the Dred Scott Decision, which asserts that a slave is not a citizen.

One year before Harriet Tubman escaped, suffragettes met in Seneca Falls, New York to debate whether of not women should have the right to vote. This Women's Rights Convention was led by Lucretia Mott and Elizabeth Cady Stanton. Frederick Douglas, a former slave who became an abolitionist and orator, spoke at the convention in favor of women's right to vote. However, they did not win this right in Crazy Horse's lifetime. The first country to give women that right was New Zealand, in 1893.

The Civil War began in 1861.

During Crazy Horse's lifetime, the world saw the invention of the sewing machine by Elias Howe in 1846; dynamite by Alfred Nobel in 1867; and the telephone by Alexander Graham Bell in 1876. Thomas Edison invented the electric lightbulb two years after Crazy Horse died.

After the Civil War, a series of wars against Native

Americans continued into the 1890s. The same year Crazy Horse died, the Nez Perce leader Chief Joseph was forced to surrender. In 1886, the same year the Statue of Liberty was dedicated in New York, the famous Apache chief Geronimo was also forced to surrender. Police arrested and killed the Sioux chief Sitting Bull on the Pine Ridge Reservation in 1890. Two weeks later, US troops killed over two hundred Sioux at the Battle of Wounded Knee. Native Americans were granted US citizenship in 1924.

When Maisie and Felix meet Crazy Horse:

The US flag had thirty-one stars for thirty-one states: Delaware, Pennsylvania, New Jersey, Georgia, Connecticut, Massachusetts, Maryland, South Carolina, New Hampshire, Virginia, New York, North Carolina, Rhode Island, Vermont, Kentucky, Tennessee, Ohio, Louisiana, Indiana, Mississippi, Illinois, Alabama, Maine, Missouri, Arkansas, Michigan, Florida, Texas, Iowa, Wisconsin, and California.

James Buchanan was elected as the fifteenth president of the United States. That same year, the twenty-eighth president, Woodrow Wilson, was born.

In Crazy Horse's lifetime, seven more states received statehood: Minnesota, Oregon, Kansas, West Virginia, Nevada, Nebraska, and Colorado.

But South Dakota, which now occupies the territory where he lived, did not become a state until 1889, over ten years after he died. That same year, North Dakota also became a state.

What was happening in other parts of the world:

Victoria was the queen of England.

Russia owned what is now Alaska (the US purchased it from them in 1867 for $7,200,000).

A potato blight in Ireland caused the Irish Potato Famine (1845–1849), which killed one million people in Ireland and led to at least another one million leaving the country.

The United States went to war with Mexico in 1846.

In 1853, Commodore Matthew Perry sailed into Tokyo, leading to the opening of trade between Japan and the United States.

In 1859, work began on the Suez Canal, which connects the Mediterranean Sea with the Red Sea through Egypt.

Continue your adventures in
The Treasure Chest!